COASTAL LIVES

MIRIAM SAGAN

CENTER Press
Santa Fe, New Mexico
1991

First Edition, December, 1991
Published by CENTER Press
307 Johnson Street
Santa Fe, NM 87501

Library of Congress Catalog Card Number 91-75996

ISBN: 0-916185-02-8

Acknowledgments
and Dedications

The first two chapters of this novel appeared as a chapbook, *Paths To The Nudist Beach (Samisdat*, 1989). Sections also appeared in *Samisdat Magazine.*

Thanks to Carol Bergé, Merritt Clifton, Tom Ireland, and Robert Winson for their help with the manuscript and to Jan Riemer for typesetting.

Thanks to Devon Miller-Duggan for showing me the Sargent; and to Judith Powsner for "women alone." And to Mark Mendel for "Pull this change."

INTRODUCTION

This book insisted I read it. By the end of the second page, I was completely drawn into a story I didn't want to put down. The writing is enticing — compact, steady and driven, taking one there without wasting gas. These elements carried me along, as if I were a hitchhiker, lucking out.

There is a feeling of wholeness in this work, related to the use of the number four — in this case, four fine sisters, at battle, in bed, beside themselves, confronting each other as siblings. Beyond this interweaving of lives, the fiction itself takes on a rounded quality, as if these people were molded out of beach clay, tossed back and forth in the hands of the maker until the form felt just right.

At the beginning of each chapter, we see the Island as through a guidebook; the commentary adds to our information without distracting from the flow of the story. Immediately, we feel the salt and sand beneath the soles of this Cape Cod encounter, and by the end of the nude beach scene which opens the book, Sagan's confident, casual tone makes me feel that she'd be a great friend to drive across country with or to talk away the night on a darkened porch.

As in much modern fiction, this work probably lies somewhere on the bend between autobiography and fantasy, yet we don't need to know what did or did not actually happen. It's difficult to guess which sister Ms. Sagan identifies with. The least likely would be the youngest, Cathy "with her condo and her new car and sailing club and a desk at the bank with her name on it and her investments and her three-piece suits and her dresser drawer full of lacy underwear. Certainly she was the only one of the family who really acted like an adult woman." Though Sagan claims that Cathy shares a "narrow but fierce recklessness" with her sisters, she seems to be more a precursor to the yuppie mentality of the eighties.

Matty, the mother of the four girls, is a wonderful presence, like an axis or an Island signpost. She doesn't dominate the lives of her daughters, possibly because she has lived her own life fully and found it "delicious."

Elizabeth, the dark, seductive daughter with a clear voice of her own, is second only to the lost, lovely Mary, who has left her husband and not yet found herself. Her state of dislocation and deflation is well-conveyed: she has that lethargy of spirit that makes it difficult for her to find anything worth wearing, but men find her sadness irresistible.

Mary's path is the most complex in the book; she doesn't quite have a grip on herself, as she floats from a one-night stand with a married drummer to a female lover from her Women's Group. In the latter scene, the tentativity of a strange, new tenderness is delicately balanced with feelings of reservation.

In contrast to Mary's experiments, Therese, sister Number Three, is tall, bold, beautiful, and gay. Sisters Number One and Two imagine she keeps a wrench on her bedside table rather than KY Jelly. Therese is the kind of woman who might write on a Cambridge bathroom wall, "REAL WOMEN DON'T EAT MEN." When she's faced with a possible move to California: "She insisted that she loved scrod, whatever that was, and did not feel alive if she wasn't within walking distance of the Atlantic, and smoke-filled rooms where proper Boston dykes fought over socialist-feminism."

Wonderfully diverse, these four souls finally join together to have tea at the Copley Plaza at the end of the book. Such a reunion seems remarkable and yet as believable as their idyllic Island childhood, playing Spud, lying down in a bed of pine needles, or finding that garden made for viewing the moon.

I particularly like the childhood image of the four of them "cramming themselves together under the picnic table in the backyard. There, sweltering in the heat, they would make up dialogue about how they were slowly freezing to death as the stove went out and the drifts of snow piled higher." Sagan retains that early imagination which makes anything possible. The writing is fresh, not over-worked, full of candor, free and easy, wheeling us along, moving from the college streets of Boston to the wide-open Southwest. The Southwest chapter does lend a nice contrast to New-Age New England, which has one foot in the future, with Patti Smith, and one foot in the past with John Singer Sargent.

The fads of an era are reflected in the books that each sister reads. One only has tomes with the word "Zen" in the title, and Sagan's so much of-the-times tone often resonates with a touch of embarrassment, for suddenly we realize our own journey through that decade might not have been so unique. The humor always does have a bit of an edge to it. "But at least we know we're better off here than our grandmothers were, sitting around in the potato famine eating thin gruel or something and dying in childbirth every minute and a half."

More than a document of the Seventies or a personal history, we are given a work of art that is worth living with because it's more than life, transporting us to those moments when the world seems to spin yet stop. By the end of the novel, we return to one of those places, a graveyard filled with sunflowers where Mary lies down. "The field was in the center of the Island; the Island was in the center of the ocean, in the middle of the blue sea full of sharks and whales, treasure and shipwreck, drowned sailors and microscopic protozoa. She lay in the center of everything and felt the field turn toward the sun . . ." Her own center retrieved, her solitude accepted, I am left feeling very well-satisfied with this piece of short fiction and with life itself. I have to remind myself there's nothing wrong with feeling that good.

— Laura Chester
Alford, Massachusetts
July, 1991

vii

Chapter I

Seen from the air, the Island resembles a dolphin or leaping fish; lying sea-suckled on all sides, four or five miles off the Cape, southeast, in the Atlantic. The Island is the largest of a group that includes another good-sized tourist community, a speckling of small green islands, sparsely inhabited and named for an English queen, and Noman's: a waterless rock inhabited only by wind and gulls and bombed mercilessly by the Army for target practice.

Glaciers, the ice age in motion, came out of the north and ground the continent flat. The glaciers left New England stony, planted the fields with gigantic boulders that no force since — human, beast, or machine — has ever attempted to remove. They left Pleistocene deposits on the Island, complex drifts that the archaeologists label Illinoian, with outwashes of older sediments from the old coastal plain, foundation of the Island.

Like all islands, this one seeded itself from the mainland. First, birds, then a spider on a leaf, a snake on a log, seeds airborne and waterborne, seeds hidden in the guts of animals, and eventually the climax community: oak, beech, hickory, white cedar, black cherry, cranberry, beach plum, and even grape.

T HE BATHERS LAY NAKED on the sand along the water's edge. Warmed by sun, they turned on their beach towels or leapt up and ran into the ocean's spray, tumbling with the waves. Men and women lay chastely side by side, families picnicked in the shade of the cliff, a woman posed for her lover's camera in an architectural niche, and children built a sandcastle just out of reach of the oncoming tide.

A few adventurers found a deposit of grey clay where the cliff was eroded by the waves. They smeared their naked bodies with clay, painted moons and spirals on their faces, until they resembled the mud dancers of a vanished tribe. A tourist in Bermuda shorts pretended to look seaward, trying not to stare at the naked dancers. Down along the stretch of white beach, two figures were flying a kite high in the air; the multicolored dragon tail streamed against the endless blue of sky.

Muriel's children sat on the nudie beach. Elizabeth recognized them, even though she hadn't seen them in years. Elizabeth had come to the beach for a purpose beyond that of the usual exhibitionism or voyeurism: she had come for the status of an all-over full body tan. As she did not intend to socialize she was armed with a large book, a larger straw hat, a bottle of lotion, and a thermos of iced tea. She was also armed with truisms about the nudie beach, developed during the years of sunbathing with her sisters. They'd started coming to the beach at puberty, years ago, when it was still appropriately called Jungle Beach and could be reached only by an overland hike. Now it was part of the public beach and could be reached by a stroll past some large rocks, the agreed upon demarcation line. The truisms about the nudie beach were: Oh, it's nice to see whole families together. It's nice to see older couples. It's nice to see children and even little babies toddling about in the surf. Only Therese, the next to youngest sister, had once collapsed in laughter, saying, "Look at all the penises!" And after that, Elizabeth couldn't help but notice herself noticing them. The central myth about the nudie beach was that it was sensual, not sexual. This was a lie, however, evinced by the fact that you always wanted to fuck your brains out after an afternoon on the nudie beach, or at least Elizabeth did, although she had never dared to corroborate this with her sisters.

But today she was here alone, without the protective screen of her three sisters, and she was noticing Muriel's children sitting together on a bright beach towel. She hadn't seen either brother or sister since before Muriel had died. When was that? It had been at least a dozen or so years ago, and she'd been almost sixteen, so Jed must have been seventeen, and she'd had a bit of a crush on him. She peeked over at Jed now. He looked handsome, with a hooked nose and a lot of black curly hair. Elizabeth liked Jewish men; the man she was living with was Jewish. It worried her that if she broke his heart it might be considered anti-Semitic. Jed looked good, tall and tan, but his sister, what was her name, Laurel, looked terrible. Her ribs stuck out, she was yellow, her stringy hair was in her face and she was staring down at the sand. Elizabeth couldn't really remember much about Laurel. As a child she'd been shy but sweet. Maybe Muriel's death had hit Laurel the hardest. She'd only been eleven at the time; it was hard for a girl to lose her mother.

The afternoon Muriel had died, Elizabeth and her older sister Mary had been playing with Barbie dolls that ostensibly belonged to their younger sisters. Although they were too old for dolls, they were enjoying dressing up Skipper, Barbie's little sister, in Barbie's clothes, so that she would look like a French whore. Their father came in and told them to be quiet; their mother Matty was lying down with a headache and weeping because her best friend Muriel had died. Mary had expected it, knowing about the cancer and the numerous operations, but Elizabeth managed to be surprised. It hadn't really occurred to Elizabeth that someone's mother could die, although of course her own mother's mother was dead, and her father's, too. Mary and Elizabeth became very quiet, and they stopped dressing up

3

Skipper and left her with contorted arms and legs, dressed in a sheer black body stocking, on the coffee table.

Elizabeth squinted up in the hot sun and then looked squarely over at Jed. He was smiling at her. She walked over and squatted down in the sand next to him. "Hi," she said, looking straight into his brown eyes and giving him her hand. "I thought I recognized you." He smiled at Laurel, who didn't look up. "Want to come in the water?" asked Elizabeth, as if she were a hostess and the beach and sea were hers to offer. Jed followed her into the surf. It was a mild day and the swells passed them at waist level and then rolled easily toward shore.

"How's your family?" asked Jed. "And your mother, how is she doing these days? I heard about your father . . . I'm sorry."

"Fine. Everyone's fine. My mother seems to be doing pretty well, although I was worried when she retired. She's always been so active, you know. But now she's spending the winters down in the Caribbean and she also seems to be getting interested in real estate. Maybe it will be a second career. I guess she's adjusted to my father's death, but it's hard to tell. We don't talk much. Baby Cathy is the closest to her, I guess. But basically everyone's fine. So what are you doing with yourself? Living on the Island?

"No, I'm living in Cambridge. I'm in graduate school."

"Really! Me too. I'm practically living in Harvard Square."

"Well, I'm in Cambridgeport, off of Western Avenue down near the river. The whole neighborhood is grungy, but it can be pleasant, too. Where are you studying?"

"At Harvard, I'm embarrassed to admit." She laughed. Of course she was not embarrassed at all, she was boasting.

"I'm in the Comparative Lit department. My family thinks I'm a bum. They don't believe I can read five languages. I think my mother's actually convinced that I'm unemployed; no matter how many times I tell her about my teaching fellowship, my students, she just looks at me blankly. Maybe she thinks I'm just a slow undergraduate instead of someone who has almost finished a Ph.D. dissertation on Proust." Here, she was boasting again, and why? Well, Jed looked beautiful, spray clinging to his chest, squinting a bit near-sightedly with big brown eyes. "And you?" she asked. "Where and what are you studying?"

4

"I'm in sociology at B.U. My father seems quite pleased, actually. I think he's glad to have a scholar in the family, the icing on the cake after he was forced to go into business to make a living."

"How is your father? Did I hear he'd remarried? I hope this isn't too personal, but is it all right with you, after your mother and all?"

"Yes. It feels okay. I think he's happy, and that's the most important thing, of course. After Muriel's death I was afraid I'd have to take care of him, maybe even move back in the house. I wasn't sure how helpless he would be, but he recovered, after time. As to the new wife, it's strange. She can hardly feel like a stepmother. She's not much older than we are and has four kids."

They shook their heads together. Jed took both her hands in his and they jumped a particularly large wave. His hands were surprisingly big, slender, and brown, and warm. She smiled at him, stupidly forgetting to speak, and wishing wildly that a wave would throw her against his chest so she could kiss him. Then she recovered her social graces: "And how is your sister?"

"Not too good," he said, "she's had . . ."

Anorexia, Elizabeth added in her own mind. Or too much speed. But Jed just said: "A mental breakdown."

"I'm sorry," she said.

"So am I," he said, looking right at her.

"Do you want to screw?" asked Elizabeth, without thinking, shocked more by her language than her daring. It seemed like the most natural thing in the world.

Jed laughed. "Here?"

"No," she said, "there," waving vaguely toward shore.

"I know a place," he said slowly, and took her hand. He led her out of the water and back across the beach. He waved at his sister, but didn't seem concerned about leaving her. He led Elizabeth through a maze of sunbathers and beach blankets, children and dogs, back to where the sand ended and the salt pond began. Sometimes in winter the sea rose over the beach and cut a channel to the pond, but in summer it was warm and briny, and full of eel grass. "Can you swim it?" he asked. "It's not too deep but the bottom is kind of muddy and too slippery to stand in."

5

She could swim it. They paddled across the estuary and came to the deserted farther shore. A few feet into the pine forest, and they were completely hidden from view. Jed grabbed her but he didn't kiss her at first. They held each other very tightly, cold at first, and salty, then warm.

"I live with someone," she said.

"So do I."

She dropped down to the bed of sand and pine needles and pulled him on top of her. His curly hair was in her mouth and eyes. He kissed her belly and she shuddered. She put her tongue in his mouth. He came into her. After a while she started moaning and he kissed her to quiet her; someone might hear. But then she came under him and he forgot about being quiet.

When they were done, they stood up. Jed had to repress a desire to shake himself all over like a dog. He wanted to say: you know, in Japan women put their hair in their mouths so they won't yell when they come. Absurdly, he wanted Elizabeth to marry him. At that moment, he thought they would do very well as husband and wife. But instead he just grinned and said with insane politeness, "Thank you, that was very nice."

"It was very nice," said Elizabeth and went around a small bush to pee. She squatted carefully, avoiding poison ivy. When she came back he was still smiling.

And then she said what she had wanted to say all along: "I'm sorry that your mother is dead."

*

The house lay long and low in the wooded scrub. Beyond the dusty green of oak and stunted pine glimmered the far blue of the cove and the farthest blue of sky. Matty looked out on the five acres on the Cove and knew, in her hands, her feet, and her stomach that it was hers. Here at last was the house on the hill she had always wanted, not only wanted but dreamed of, planned for, and attained, not just an old beach cottage, but designed, marked by her, an extension of her body, her monument.

North light ran the length of the house, the windowed side that opened on the cove. The glass and screened doors slammed resoundingly shut in the wind if not propped open with large beach stones. The house opened with a pantry for wet boots and sandy sneakers, hung with yellow foul weather gear, peculiarly striped umbrellas, and an assortment of straw hats, of both the chic and ridiculous variety. The kitchen and dining room flowed into each other in the open modern style, and were paved in soft red tiles from Mexico. An exposed brick fireplace stood free of the wall and marked off the area designated as the living room. The couches were beige, the walls stark white, the beams were unpainted and showed cracks as the house settled into itself.

Off this airy space, in its own wing of the house, was the master bedroom and bath, high-ceilinged and pale, cluttered with the details of habitation: framed photographs, unanswered letters, ceramic vases, unpaid bills, strewn towels, cosmetic clutter, old magazines, empty glasses, ashtrays full of pins and paper clips, postcards taped to mirrors, souvenirs of hot countries, and piles of loose change.

The opposite wing held a smaller bedroom, the official guest room which, in the absence of guests, was a catchall for ironing board, television, sewing machine, broken radio, unfolded laundry, and off season clothes. As if an afterthought, a narrow flight of stairs ran up into the attic room: a crazy quilt of eaves and corners, but with well-set dormer windows. An old-fashioned bed, with a painted white metal frame, dominated the space. On its patchwork quilt, a large calico cat lay asleep in the summer sun.

Matty picked up a coffee mug left by one of the girls, placed a coaster under it, and sighed. No matter how many times she told them, they never learned: the birch-wood table would stain. Maybe they were too spoiled to appreciate caring for fine things. Al had known how to care properly for things, but he was dead and had never seen the house, although he'd seen the initial plans three years ago. Al was dead and she'd retired. She didn't know what to do with her life anymore. She was fifty-one, a youngish widow — youngish, she *hoped*, anyway — and an ex-business woman. They had done fabulously with the store, she could be proud of that. It had been her canniness, realizing that real estate values on the island would skyrocket, that it would become a prime resort area. She had parlayed the small family supermarket into a fortune, watching the tourists' tastes and trends, adding expensive luxury items, the imported coffee, the rich cheeses, the exotic and pickled items in tins and jars. She stocked only the freshest vegetables, the largest, most perfect fruit, and her care had paid, more than paid, for her dreams and hopes.

Matty picked a yellow leaf from one of the big hanging ferns and sighed again. She'd come far, very far indeed, from the stifling triple-decker in the wrong part of Boston. Al had always uncharitably called her family "somewhere between pig-shit and lace-curtain Irish," but he was from Portland of course, and only a quarter Irish himself, with a maternal grandmother from Italy, and the rest a usual hybrid of English, Dutch, and German. "I'm a real mongrel," he would say, but he was a fair handsomish man, and Matty's mother claimed he looked pure Irish. She did hate to think of her mother, though, that narrow, bitter woman. Just a thought of her made Matty's throat constrict. She was glad they were long dead, her mother and father, but the guilty thought propelled her up for a fresh cup of coffee.

"You have four lovely daughters." She heard Muriel's voice in her head, as she so often did. Muriel — was she really dead these dozen years? That was a long time, but the hurt never truly faded, only went further back somehow, where it was harder to touch but where it kept on aching. Muriel and Matty. How well they'd gotten on, and yet Muriel had been a strange friend for her — she was Jewish, and even though she was a social worker she took certain things for granted: enough money, education. And Muriel had been one of the summer people, doomed to be a perpetual stranger no matter how many years she visited.

Maybe this is what made them friends, for Matty would always be an outsider too, never a true Islander. Muriel had been an earthy woman, with a low, wicked laugh, and she was the first, the only person that Matty had confided to about Al's ways in bed. "It lasts a second, and then he rolls over and goes to sleep," she'd giggled, and Muriel giggled too, but there was pity underneath it. Now, it was she who pitied Muriel, who was horribly dead after all, of breast cancer, of everywhere cancer, of cigarettes, at forty.

Matty did have four lovely daughters, named hopefully for saints: Mary, Elizabeth, Therese, Catherine. Four girls, and she'd certainly had them in a hurry, despite Al's perfunctory way in bed; they were now aged twenty-six, twenty-seven, twenty-eight, and twenty-nine. They thought she didn't understand, couldn't understand, but she knew, could see right through them, with their sex and their boyfriends and their plump lazy smiles and limbs. They were beautiful, every one, three almost-blondes and Elizabeth, that dark Celtic Irish, with green eyes and lightly freckled creamy skin. And they were voluptuous, like she. Therese was the real beauty of the batch: the statuesque one, the blondest hair, the bluest eyes. Not that their nice looks or advantages had gotten them anywhere. Despite Harvard and nice wardrobes, there was not a doctor or a lawyer among them. Mary had come home and married an Island carpenter with gold teeth. Matty just couldn't understand it. It wasn't even as if Mary had settled in and had a brood of children. She just seemed to float aimlessly from one job to another, mostly restaurant work, beneath her, really. Cathy, the baby, might go far. Of all of them, only she showed any drive or ambition, and a head for business. She'd been Al's favorite and knew it. Maybe the extra attention had helped — and now she was engaged, although there'd been all that fuss about the ring.

And if only a ring was the problem with Therese; no one actually told her but she wasn't a fool, she knew what it meant, tall Therese, the only skinny one, with her cropped hair, living with a woman who drove a truck. In Matty's old neighborhood there was a name for women like that, and it wasn't a pleasant name at all. How had Therese turned out like that? Why her, and not the others? She'd had plenty of boyfriends in high school, and even now if she'd only make herself agreeable, many men would be glad to have her. Was it something Matty had done, or not done, as a mother? But how could it be? She, Matty, hardly knew about such things. Perhaps it was just a sign of Therese's willfullness, something she'd done out of spite. And Elizabeth, somehow she always managed to skip over Elizabeth, almost as if Elizabeth wasn't

9

really one of her own. She even looked different, and she was mysterious, closed and deep. Elizabeth was the stranger, and Matty did not want to think about her. She sighed then, and got up for a carton of coffee ice cream, even if it was only ten-thirty in the morning.

Matty knew that her daughters talked about her behind her back. They said she needed a man. Even Therese agreed. But then they didn't know, and she didn't plan to tell them, that she'd had a man, down in the Caribbean last winter, a grey-haired handsome gentleman of an appropriate age who had a boat that slept four and who could dance. And dance they did, and sleep on the boat that was fine for two; and she had allowed him to make love to her, first from curiosity and then from real passion. He'd fallen rather in love with her, which was sad, at least for him, because she couldn't feel anything in the place where she knew her heart should be. Perhaps it was too soon after Al's death, he'd condoled. But it wasn't that, she was sure, only a strangeness in that her body felt warm in a way it never had before and yet her heart felt nothing at all. Did she have a heart? She suspected she did. And she had a small emerald ring from the gentleman with the boat, who lived in California and had never been to Boston. It was special, the ring, for emeralds were her favorite stone and green her favorite color, she loved anything that was green, including this modest gem cut from Brazilian mines. Matty knew she could meet her gentleman friend again this winter if she liked, but she didn't tell her daughters.

She finished off the ice cream and went to brew another cup of coffee. She was sick of that decaffeinated stuff. This would be real coffee. She wished Muriel were alive. She would have liked telling her about the cabin of the boat that was neatly made of polished wood and about the multicolored lights strung up in the harbor that cast a necklace of jewels out on the water.

Before Elizabeth went back to the city, to the hot Monday that awaited her, and the meeting with her advisor, she made a duplicate key to her mother's house on the cove. "Make a key," Matty had urged, "so you can use the house when I'm not here. Come up in the winter, if you like, have some friends up for the weekend. I won't be here Labor Day, either."

On the screen door was posted a sign in Matty's clear greengrocer handwriting: DO NOT LET THE CAT OUT. The cat was a strange one, with markings that gave it the look of having a mustache, and it had only three legs. A customer had found it at the dump, and in a completely uncharacteristic fit of soft-heartedness Matty had adopted it. Its single back leg had grown unusually strong, to compensate. And it was a good mouser, although the effect was more like a cross between a rabbit and a three-legged stool than like a springing cat.

Elizabeth was testing the key in the lock, and Mary was companionably chatting at her, holding the screen door open, when the calico cat made a wild ecstatic leap into escape, running off toward the woods, but stopping to roll in the dirt, happy. Mary, the careless warden, laughed guiltily, but Elizabeth, knowing she would be blamed, snapped: "Catch him!" The two sisters half dashed, half ambled after the cat, but only succeeded in driving him into the woods. It was hot, and they would have all liked to lie in the shade, but the cat was fueled by some feline necessity, while the women were only perspiring in pursuit. He vanished in an orange flash, and they stood knee-deep in poison ivy, creepers, scrub pines, and oak.

"It's nice out here," said Elizabeth, but then she provoked a quarrel.

"I'm glad the cat got away," said Mary, breathing hard and laughing.

"You would, you're such a hippie. Someone around here has to be the responsible one. I don't know how you manage. Matty will blame me, of course, because she knows I'm responsible, and you'll get off again, even though you were careless."

Mary was shocked: tears came to her eyes as if she'd been slapped. This outburst was so unlike the kind Elizabeth and yet so like the bitch Elizabeth that Mary felt frozen. She decided not to cry and took the only other available tack.

"Fuck you," she said succinctly. "Stop blaming me. It's not that important. Why are you making such a big fuss?" But then, unable to leave well enough alone, she moved from the righteous to the vituperative. "What's the matter, are you and that guy Howard fighting or something? Well, don't worry, just bring your live-in up here for the weekend and you can have a lot of sex and solve all your problems."

Mary had hit a sore spot. "Fuck you, bitch," said Elizabeth.

Mary felt better, then conciliatory. "Do you still want to go food shopping? You said you'd give me a hand with it, and we should fill up Matty's refrigerator after eating out of it so much."

"Stop badgering me," yelled Elizabeth.

"All right, Miss Responsible. Well, fuck you, anyway," finished Mary.

So Mary went for a walk on the beach by herself. After a while, she wished she had a straw hat. Every year Elizabeth got a new straw hat for the beach. This year it had been a chic number in black and white weave, but the year before had been Mary's favorite, with straw-colored silk flowers tied on the back with streamers.

Mary squatted down to piss in the ocean, discreetly moving the crotch of her bathing suit an inch or so out of the way. Then she walked again. Loosely scattered along the surf, bathers hurled themselves into a pastel meeting of water and air. Mary wore shell earrings and a matching necklace. She carried her purple sneakers tied over one shoulder. Her black bathing suit was frayed, even transparent in patches, and she felt a little fat, exposed on the beach. But then a middle-aged woman with an older husband passed Mary, walking in the opposite direction. The woman glanced at Mary, appraising, jealous. Mary felt gorgeous in her black bathing suit.

She was happy, yet some tension nagged at her. Maybe it was Joe. Things hadn't seemed quite right between them in the last few weeks, and yet they weren't fighting or anything. The sex was fine, too, and Mary believed sex to be the most reliable barometer of a marriage or relationship. Besides, it wasn't as if things were usually that great between her and Joe anyway. They led pretty independent lives, so probably nothing was wrong.

She walked along the widening low-tide spread of beach: salt marsh and stone wall to the right, open ocean on her left. She passed dogs and frisbee throwers. A plump fair-haired woman came toward her out of the faint mist, and she felt sure it was her mother in an aqua-skirted suit. But it wasn't, nor was the other woman, lean and black-haired, striding along, her mother's best friend, dead by this woman's age, years ago.

Turning toward home, Mary saw that Elizabeth had come down to the beach, too. She was glimmering in the salt light, in a white dress that blew about her bare legs, wearing a straw hat out of an Impressionist picnic; they smiled at each other, lifting their hands up to wave.

Their mother saw them as they came up the path to the house, laughing and talking. "He didn't," she heard one of them exclaim, and then giggle. Well, at least they seemed to be getting on better these days; they'd fought so much as children. They let the screen door slam but she offered them some coffee, the real coffee she had just brewed.

*

Elizabeth was the only one of the sisters to have properly admired Cathy's ring. "What a pretty diamond," she'd said, although she thought it rather ostentatious, and garishly set with small emeralds. "Thank you," gushed Cathy. She was the first sister to have gotten engaged. Mary might be married, but she'd had a horrible hippie wedding and no diamond ring.

Elizabeth was supposed to be kind to Cathy. It was part of the family construct. It had begun because Mary and Therese, the first and third sisters, were genuinely fond of each other, which had left Elizabeth and Cathy to round out the Little Womanish symmetry. Elizabeth had her strongest feelings for Mary, love and hate mixed together with an odd sort of protectiveness, as if Mary were the younger and she the elder sister. Elizabeth tolerated Cathy, and even liked her, but she hated Therese. She was no longer sure why she hated Therese, yet she had accumulated a lot of evidence over the years. They lived within a few blocks of each other in Cambridge, but never saw each other, by choice or by accident.

"You should have heard what Therese said when she saw the ring!" exclaimed Cathy. She was beginning to look perfectly manicured, thought Elizabeth with dislike. Her clothes were manicured, although in incontrovertible good

taste and of the best natural fibers; her apartment was manicured, although with an enviable view of the river; her job was
manicured, although this was enviable only if you liked banks;
and her fiance was manicured — and here the envy stopped,
for Elizabeth despised hulking blond preppy bankers.

"What did Therese say?"

"She said, 'Gee, I wouldn't want to get hit with that.' "

"Her rape work is going to her head."

"I'd think she'd be glad to get raped."

"Cathy!" Now even Elizabeth was shocked by her bitchiness. "Rape is no joke," she said priggishly, and took her leave.

When she was gone, Cathy looked out over the moody
river. Dusk was falling and the lights were beginning to light
up, a few sailboats turned home, the water shimmered like a
bolt of blue-violet silk. The mirrored tower of the John
Hancock building took on the color of dusk, and glimmered
slightly with the awakening lights of the city at night. Cathy
took off her diamond ring and held it carefully to the window
pane — the condo was hers, after all — and with it she
scratched in the letters of her maiden name.

Therese bicycled home from the center late that night. She
was wary in the darkness. Anything could happen —
muggers, rapists, a stick between the spokes of her bicycle.
The square was completely deserted, except for the eternal
construction sites: the piles of cinder blocks, the stilled
machines, the traffic barriers now painted with slogans and
murals. As Therese pedaled rapidly she thought of Lu. Maybe
she would have left her some dinner. Lu liked to cook huge
pots of odd concoctions, curries and spicy vegetable stews;
in this heat she would dress in a pair of gauze harem pants.
Lu still seemed very exotic to Therese, even if they had been
living together for over two years. Lu was half Japanese.
She'd gone to UC Berkeley during the riots. Her real name
was not Lu, and she was rich, or her family was, but she did
not allow Therese to indulge in her inclination to play
working-class hero.

At the red light, the lit-up window of a chic shoe store
caught Therese's eye. In it a woman mannequin was bound
and gagged, with nothing on but a black lace teddy and a pair
of backless "fuck me" stiletto highheeled shoes. A man, also
of plastic, was walking on her with cowboy boots. The bound

woman seemed to be looking at Therese. Slowly, she got off the bicycle and looked closely at the window. For a still moment, she and the bound woman stared into each other's faces. Then Therese picked up a brick from a pile at one of the ubiquitous construction sites and weighed it in her hand. It felt good, good and heavy. Then she sent the brick crashing through the plate glass window.

Toward morning, Mary had a disturbing dream, in which she was trying to make love to a man who looked like her husband but kept turning into someone else: a man who looked nothing like her husband, and then a stranger who might have been a woman. She woke herself in the pale dawn, turning to where Joe should be in bed, but not finding him. He was not in the shack, and the old beat-up blue VW, originally her car, was gone. It didn't look as if he had come home that night at all. Maybe he was out fucking that bitch Molly Taylor, but more likely he was just drunk or rambling around. The house was a mess, sand in the bed, mussel shells in the sink, laundry on the furniture, roaches in the ashtray, dust mice in the corner, ants on the table, books on the floor.

She washed her face and brushed her teeth. She felt desolate. She couldn't stand the sight of the dirty cabin. Light was just beginning to flood the sky. She went out onto the porch and locked the door behind her, something that was hardly ever done on the Island. She thought: I'll hitchhike down to the ferry, I'll go to Boston and stay with Therese. I'll become a lesbian, I'll have lots of lovers, no, I'll go to California and join a commune, I'll go to Japan and teach English, I'll go to China and learn ancient potting techniques, I'll . . . She saw the boogie board leaning up against the shack . . . I'll hitchhike up-island and go surfing off the cliffs at dawn.

Mary cradled her warm house-key in her palm. Then she dug a little hole in the sand and buried it. She shouldered the board and walked to the road. She faced down-island and put out her thumb, her back to the dark belly of the Island, the cliffs, the open surf beyond, the great swell of the Atlantic, where she was going.

15

Chapter II

Next to come to the Island were the Indians, part of the Algonquin group; tribute tribes to those on the mainland, their name meant "land surrounded by bitter water." They were also called, variously, "the land or place of the people who harbor others," and "the refugee place." Living in bee-hived dwellings constructed of saplings and mats, they also shared a community long house. These first people cultivated corn, beans, peas, squash, and tobacco; they planted a herring for fertilizer in each seed hill. They also ate, as did those who came after them, lobsters, crabs, oysters, clams, quahogs, swordfish, and bass.

The first European colonists found these Native Americans courteous and gentle, tall and black-haired, wearing little in the summer, deerskin by winter. Adultery was considered the worst sin among them, although fornication before marriage was no sin

17

at all. Their gods were those of the four directions; the favorite god was from the southwest, the wind of good weather.

In the beginning, the creator made a woman and a man of stone, which he then smashed into pieces. Next, he made a woman and man out of a tree; these were our first ancestors. There was also the story of the ugly Indian girl who fell in love with an eel, an eel who later turned back into a handsome prince. The names of these people also mean: "The people with the eastland ancestors who are the light of day."

"I think you should marry me," Jed said to Elizabeth. He was extremely angry, and his low voice shook.

"You're just saying that to bother me," she retorted, also angry, and chain-smoking low-tar cigarettes. Elizabeth seldom smoked. Jed was smoking too, unfiltered Camels, and the oddly erotic sight of the two packs of cigarettes nestled together on the table further enraged Elizabeth.

They were sitting in the Cafe Pamplona, in the cozy below street-level light, the haze of smoke, and clouds of steam from the espresso machine. Anyone looking at them but unable to hear their conversation would have thought of them as a charming, typically Cambridge couple. Next to them, at one of the cramped round tables, two undergraduates were discussing Kant. Elizabeth noticed that their complexions were bad. Her own complexion was good, but soon to be ruined by the conversation, the smoke, and the large piece of chocolate almond cake that she had anxiously ordered.

"I love you," said Jed, lowering his voice melodramatically.

"You don't even know me."

"I know you."

"Having sex with a person once does not constitute 'knowing' them. Besides, I'm living with someone and I thought you were too."

"I was, but it couldn't last. She was a member of the Socialist Workers Party and was sick of cohabitating with a white male oppressor. Besides, the Party was about to transfer her to New York."

Elizabeth laughed despite herself. She wished things could be as simple between her and Howard, whose faults were not

18

limited to obvious political ones. "Why do you want to marry me?" she said. "Apart from the fact that our mothers were best friends and that I screwed you on the beach once?"

"You're the first woman I ever wanted to marry. Let's do it. We're perfect for each other."

"I'm not sure if I should be flattered or insulted," said Elizabeth.

"Well, if you won't marry me, at least go away with me for Labor Day."

Elizabeth hesitated. This was the kind of offer that actually tempted her. Cambridge was sweltering under a heat wave, her live-in, Howard, had been acting remote and even a little peculiar, and somehow the fact that Jed had reduced his offer from matrimony to a weekend trip proved his seriousness to her. In any case, she loved the words, "go away."

"Where?" she asked.

"Oh, the Island, where else? We could stay in a nice guest house I know of in the Harbor. Unfortunately, the lease will be up on the house my father was renting."

"The Harbor will be such a mob scene on Labor Day, though. No, wait a minute, my mother should be gone that weekend. She's supposed to go to somebody's wedding in Portland, or something. I'm sure we could stay there. The house is gorgeous, and besides, I just made a spare key."

Jed stubbed out his cigarette and resolved to stop smoking. Cancer ran in his family. It was suicidal, and besides, now he had something to live for. It was as if, before he had met Elizabeth, he had lived for ideas, some sense of himself that was created by ideas. He wanted to be a good teacher, a humane one, who could help his students question the systems under which they lived. He ecologically rode his bicycle, put in his hours at the food co-op, shared the housework, respected women. But this had a hollow center, a center he felt filling in Elizabeth's presence; she made a warm pool of light in his chest where before there had been a faint ache around his beating heart.

"Okay," he said. "We'll go to your mother's. Labor Day." He stuck out his hand, and she shook it formally.

"So when will you marry me?" he asked.

19

"On the Fourth of July! Now leave me alone!" She swept her things into her bag and ran out into the street, met by the swelter of oven-hot air and the noisy exhaust of traffic.

Elizabeth was glad to go to the Island. It was the thought of Jed that panicked her. In the week before Labor Day she could locate no one who could help her locate herself. Her shrink was out of town, hobnobbing on the beach with everyone else's shrink and spending Elizabeth's money. Not that Elizabeth begrudged her shrink, whom she adored. When Elizabeth first set out in search of formal therapeutic help, she hadn't set the usual criteria as to training and fees. She wanted only a woman at least ten years older than herself who was happily married and had good taste. On their first meeting the shrink had said, "What a lovely sweater," and Elizabeth was hooked; it was a lovely sweater, being both mauve and angora, with pearl buttons.

Cathy was also out of town, gone to the Hamptons with friends of her boring fiance. It seemed ridiculous to go in search of sand and waves beyond the Island, but the fiance was from New York, and perhaps it felt more like home. This left Elizabeth with only her most ancient resource: her sister Mary. But on the phone Mary had sounded worse than Elizabeth.

"I've left Joe. Or rather, he's left me. It's fine. He's moved in with that bitch. I'm fine. I've got back my old job, baking pies. Oh, hell, Elizabeth, I wish I was dead," she said, and burst into hysterical tears. Elizabeth calmed her, telling herself that it was all for the best, as Joe was an unreformed asshole and Mary a marvelous and creative woman, deserving of more. Mary stopped crying eventually under these blandishments, but Elizabeth no longer had the heart to discuss her own problems.

For this reason no one warned her and she did not warn herself of the approaching storm in Howard. He had been acting odd and withdrawn even before her encounter with Jed, but in the following weeks he closed into himself, into his library cubicle, and had taken to sleeping on the couch so he "wouldn't disturb" her when he came home late at night. As a result, Elizabeth had barely seen him of late.

Elizabeth was neatly packing up her overnight bag, folding the clothes on the bed; she had told Howard that she was weekending at her mother's house with her sisters. "Then why," he demanded, "are you taking your diaphragm?" He must have checked the medicine cabinet and found it gone from its habitual place alongside the Clinique soap and the bottle of vitamin C tablets.

"Oh, just in case," she said breezily.

"Just in case what?"

"Howard, you don't own me."

Howard picked up the first solid object that came to hand, which in this case was the hideously expensive and high tech amplifier from the sound system, and hurled it out the window. The window was closed; later Elizabeth realized he must have thought it was open. Glass shattered wildly. The amplifier crashed and crumbled, scattering gravel in the courtyard below. Everything seemed to be in slow motion, and Howard came toward Elizabeth, also in slow motion, and punched her in the eye with moderate force. She wheeled very calmly, picked up her bag, and walked out of the apartment. It was cooling toward evening. The leaves were still green in the lamp light of dusk. Elizabeth did not cry, even as her eye began to swell. She knew it would be a bruiser. She'd gotten a black eye once before, in the third grade, playing "Red rover, red rover, let green come over" and she'd been wearing a green sweater with red leaves on it and she'd run for it, straight into the bullet-shaped head of one of her classmates with a Scotch-Irish last name.

Elizabeth did not cry now. She counted her possessions: credit cards, cash, bank book, keys, diaphragm, bathing suit, underwear. Her books and clothes were at Howard's. The lease was in his name. She counted her options: Howard was a psychopath and she couldn't remember why she had lived with him for a year and a half; Cathy was out of town; she had nowhere to sleep. Her office? She was afraid Howard would stalk her. A motel? Too expensive. Her friends wouldn't be back in town until after Labor Day. She'd left her address book at Howard's, and didn't have Jed's number or address; luckily, they'd agreed to meet at the bus. I should just admit it and go to the shelter for battered women, she thought grimly, but exaggeration comforted her, and then she remembered Therese.

Therese, her sister, whom she hated, who hated her, but who lived around the block and had probably seen many battered women before. Therese, who would probably not criticize Elizabeth personally but only for her heterosexuality: not for picking the wrong man but for picking a man at all. Elizabeth turned down Therese's quiet street. Curtainless open windows leaked yellow light, the spicy smell of cooking, radio music, low quarreling. Children rode their bicycles in manic circles on the asphalt. Crickets. Sound barrier breaking with a low-flying plane. The front door of the wooden building was open, a sagging porch, mailboxes in Portuguese. So Therese had a roommate, or a lover, there were two names on her mailbox. Elizabeth walked down the hall that smelled faintly of cat piss and less faintly of stew. She knocked on the door.

"Come in, it's open."

Elizabeth walked into the bright kitchen and the startled looks of her sister and of a small Japanese woman dressed only in a pair of string bikini underpants. "Oh," all three of them said in unison, but only the Japanese woman smiled.

"Elizabeth?"

"Therese?"

"Oh my God, your eye!"

"I'm sorry."

"What happened?"

"I'm sorry to bother you, I couldn't figure out where else to go."

"It's okay."

"He hit me."

"Howard."

"First he threw the stereo amplifier out the window and then he hauled off and hit me."

"Did you provoke him?"

"Therese!" The Japanese woman sounded outraged.

"You're supposed to be a feminist," she'd said later. "How could you say something like that to your own sister, as if you were blaming her, when she was the victim?"

"You don't know Elizabeth the way I do, she's a bitch. I've often wanted to hit her," Therese had said in defense.

22

But now she said, "Oh, this is Lu. Lu, this is Elizabeth." They all looked at each other blankly. Then Lu rolled up some ice cubes in a dish towel and brought it to Elizabeth for her eye.

"Do you want to lie down?"

"No, I'll just hold it, thank you." She sank into one of their uncomfortable kitchen chairs and looked around. The kitchen had a floor of red linoleum, buckling but spotless. An enormous spice rack hung over the stove. A crude poster on the wall was emblazoned with a poem called MOUNTAIN MOVING DAY and a picture of a woman with a gun. The living room held a motley assortment of furniture, much of which Elizabeth remembered from her mother's old house, plus a television with aluminum foil on the antennas, two large black cats, the original peeling wallpaper that showed a print of blue roses, gigantic hanging plants, and a rubber tree. Everything was faded, clean, shabby, cozy, the whole effect rather pleasant.

The cats came into the kitchen to observe the visitor and rubbed themselves obligingly against Lu's bare legs.

"What are their names?" asked Elizabeth, to be polite, as she didn't really care for cats.

"Muffin and Mifune," said Therese, "for the Samurai actor and for breakfast!" She and Lu looked at each other and laughed. Elizabeth felt suddenly sad, excluded from a lovers' joke.

"But we call them both Moof," said Lu, still laughing.

"I only need to stay until tomorrow," said Elizabeth.

"You can sleep on the couch. It's fine, really," said her sister.

"Thank you."

"Are you hungry?"

"A little," she replied. It seemed crass to be hungry in such a crisis, but the kitchen was having a calming effect on her. Lu brought her a plate of curried chick peas and brown rice, with a bowl of cucumber salad. Therese brought her hot peppermint tea in a mug with a chipped handle.

The two sisters embraced awkwardly. Elizabeth still held the ice pack over her eye.

The next morning, the eye was more yellow than purple. "Howard called," said Therese. Elizabeth was impressed by his sleuthsmanship, but frightened. What if he were to track her down to rape and kill her and cut her up in pieces and throw her body down an elevator shaft?

Therese continued, "He says he has moved all your books and clothes into your office and that he never wants to see you again. Please mail him his keys and a check for $22.50 for your part of the phone bill."

"Good," said Elizabeth faintly.

At the bus station, Jed exploded into a whirlwind of suspicion and concern. "What happened. Tell me, what happened, baby?" he insisted.

Elizabeth couldn't deal with it. She let him buy the bus tickets and would only say "I'll tell you later. Now hold me." She went to sleep in his lap, scrunched up across the bus seats.

Once on the ferry, she felt safer, as if the widening gap of water between her and the mainland were further protection from Howard. The island seemed a haven. She told Jed the story slowly, in a strained voice, staring down at her own lap. When she looked up, he was crying very gently. At this sign of empathy, Elizabeth began weeping with increasing loudness, feeling her tears flow for the first time since Howard hit her, much to the interest and surprise of the other ferry passengers.

"He hit me, he hit me, that bastard, I want to kill him." And she bawled, stupid with relief.

"What would make you feel better? What can I do? What would help?"

Elizabeth looked at him, stopped mid-tear. The idea was completely novel; no one had ever asked her before what would help. And now that someone had asked, the question was left without an answer.

Jed's father had left him the Island car in the long-term parking lot, so once off the ferry they drove to Elizabeth's mother's house. From the outside, in the dark, it looked cold and uninviting. Elizabeth wondered if it had been a mistake to come at all. She felt lonely. Besides, she barely knew Jed.

Once inside, they lit the wood neatly arranged in the fireplace and turned on a few of the yellow lamps. The last moths of summer flattened themselves against the screen, drawn to the light. Shadows filled the deep corners of the furniture, and Elizabeth began to be lulled by the firelight, lulled and peaceful, but somehow detached as well, as if she were floating a few inches outside of her own skin.

Jed began to talk, soft and witty, telling her stories and jokes, even riddles, the plots to movies, his favorite books, his earliest memories, his worst fears, how he lost his virginity, the first time he tripped on acid. Elizabeth was amused and bored; she wanted to make love, and she stretched out her legs and wiggled her toes.

She sighed, and said, "Let's make love." It was easier to say than it had been the first time.

"No," he said, but he leaned over and kissed her.

"But why not? We did before. Why ever not?"

"I don't know you well enough."

"But that's completely ridiculous."

"I want to tell you all my stories first," he insisted.

She wanted to snap: your stories aren't all that great, and making love is; but she restrained herself. Actually, she did not believe him. But that night Jed climbed into bed with her only to curl up and sleep chastely on his side, even when she kissed the back of his neck.

The next morning, she awoke dissociated, as if she had made love to a stranger and awakened in an unfamiliar apartment. But Jed was tender, and smiled at her like a lover. She wavered between happiness and terror. Maybe he's gay, and afraid to tell me, or impotent, or maybe he has a disease . . . herpes or AIDS or some kind of incurable VD that is resistant to penicillin. Or maybe he just hates me. Maybe I'm ugly. But none of these seemed like a real possibility to her.

Jed remained tender and cooked her an omelette for breakfast. Just as they were sitting down to eat, the sound of a car on the gravel and shell of the driveway startled them. More startling to Elizabeth was the sight of her mother Matty, loaded with packages and carrying a bunch of yellow paper narcissus wrapped in green florist paper.

"Elizabeth!"

"Ma! I thought, I thought you were off in . . . "

"Well, I wasn't," snapped Matty, on the verge of forgetting that she had given Elizabeth a key to the house, and looking around for signs of an orgy or at least of domestic disarray, and disappointingly finding neither.

"Would you like some eggs?" asked Elizabeth in the most conciliatory tone that she could manage, considering that she was morally in the right. "With sour cream and scallions, they're very good, Jed made them."

"Jed?" said Matty, and then recognition flooded her with tenderness, and she felt as if she might weep: "My God, Jed, I haven't seen you since . . ." and she went over to him and hugged him violently. He was wearing only jeans, and his warm naked chest was both startlingly sexual and reminiscent of his childhood flesh. Why, Matty had changed his diapers, seen him toddle into the ocean his first summer at the beach, carried him up the dunes that time Muriel had been too big and pregnant with her second.

"Jed!" she exclaimed again.

"Mrs. . . ."

"Oh, call me Matty, why I remember you as a baby, and now . . . " she'd said the fond foolish thing she hadn't meant to say, and sat down abruptly at the table and began eating the plate of eggs her daughter had placed before her.

As soon as possible, Elizabeth whisked Jed off to the beach. She could not endure her mother's watchful eye, particularly over a love affair that was developing so peculiarly. All day on the beach the waves were warm, the air was cool, the beach grass fluttered in a slight wind, and around the bend some young boys were surfing on the gentle swells, and jumping off before they were carried onto the offshore rocks.

That night the Milky Way tumbled through the sky and the world was full of insects singing, crickets in the grass.

"Why don't those bugs just fuck and get it over with," mumbled Elizabeth. Her anxiety was rising at the prospect of climbing into bed with Jed, particularly as Matty had made no effort to segregate them into separate bedrooms.

Matty sat out on the deck, looking up at the stars. One of her Harvard-educated daughters had told her that a famous philosopher had said that if the stars came out to shine but once a century, all of mankind would come out to gape. Well, she, Matty, appreciated that, for she was content to come out and gape every night, if possible.

A small mist rose from the distant cove, with a wet chill in the air. Matty drew her sweater closer, her favorite red cardigan with the silver buttons. And then she saw, or thought she saw, someone standing in the mist on the edge of the deck.

The someone materialized slowly, as if not to frighten Matty, to cause her to run or scream. Matty stared steadily. Mist did not frighten her, until the mist became . . . a woman, why, it was Muriel, a pale and ghostly Muriel to be sure, but Muriel nonetheless, in a characteristic pose, with one hand on her angular hip and her chin tilted slightly forward. She was barefoot, wearing an old black tank suit and carrying a striped beach towel. Matty glanced fearfully at Muriel's chest, but both her breasts were still there, her round, medium-sized breasts that tumbled forward voluptuously, because, as usual, Muriel refused to wear a bra in the summer.

"Hello," whispered Matty.

"Hello," said Muriel, and looked at her appraisingly. She'll notice I haven't lost much weight, thought Matty, and she'll be able to tell that I'm dyeing the grey. Well, I'm a dozen years older than the last time we met, although she doesn't seem any older, in fact if anything, younger. Isn't that the way she used to wear her hair in the early fifties, when the children were little? Was it possible that the dead, instead of aging like the living, went backwards, year by year, until they were babies, and then were born again? It was an absurd thought, fitting in with neither Matty's early Catholic training nor her later conversion to her husband's cynical atheism; but the situation itself was absurd.

"You look thin," said Matty, "and pale. Are you all right? Can I get you anything? A glass of water?" It occurred to her that Muriel must have traveled a great distance, although presumably the dead could reach the Island without the aid of the Steamship Authority.

Muriel answered: "I'm fine. You look well. The house is lovely."

"Thank you, " said Matty. Behind the gentle polite words there was a great surge of emotion. She wanted to grab Muriel and demand some explanation from her, but she was afraid of frightening off the ghost, who seemed as shy as a wild creature, a rabbit or a deer.

"How are the kids?"

"They're fine," said Matty, "just fine. Jed and Elizabeth are . . . in there." Of all her daughters, she felt the least connection to Elizabeth. Mary was a tender spot of worry and aggravation, but at least she knew her. Cathy was lovely, and for Therese she felt an anger mixed with the pain of absence. Therese had been such a charming child, with curly fair hair and big eyes and an expression that made complete strangers stop in the supermarket check-out line and comment on her adorable qualities. But Elizabeth had a closed quality, some secret life of her own. No matter how friendly she was, Matty felt her to be calculating something. In some awful, hidden way, she wasn't sure if she even loved Elizabeth.

"Elizabeth and Jed?" said Muriel, smiling in wonderment.

"Yes."

"Maybe they'll make us grandmothers."

Matty smiled too. "It would be nice," she said wistfully. But then the breeze lifted, and the mist began to blow before her eyes and the image of Muriel wavered, then drifted away all at once, leaving only the crickets and the stars.

Jed and Elizabeth sat in bed. He was wearing only his underpants, which were bikinis in a peculiar shade of green. If all had been going well Elizabeth would have teased him about them, and then if things had been going really well she might have bought him some new ones. But instead she sat there mutely, wrapped up in her prettiest nightgown, hating the black negligee because it promised something Jed would not deliver. So she sulked.

"What's the matter?" asked Jed, putting his arm around her and nuzzling her shoulder.

"Nothing."

"Something is wrong. You're acting upset. What is it?"

"Nothing."

"Tell me," he demanded.

It was all too much for her, the black eye, his reserve, the unexpected appearance of her mother. She burst into tears again, exclaiming, "Why won't you make love to me?"

"I'll be back in a minute," said Jed, escaping to the bathroom. He went to brush his teeth, and caught sight of his startled, morose expression in the mirror. He squinted at himself, he was afraid, afraid of Elizabeth, of himself, of Matty. "I'm an orphan," he mumbled. But as he was not used to being afraid, he decided to disregard it.

Back in bed, he pounced on Elizabeth, whose feet had turned to ice cubes.

"No," she said.

"Yes," he said, and began kissing her, madly.

"I'm sad," she said.

"It's okay, I know," he said, and they tumbled together, finally, hot on the sheets of the guestroom bed. He came into her, and she said in rhythm: "I love you I love you I love you."

Afterward, Matty was not sure if the ghost of Muriel had been real or a dream, wish, hallucination, or the motion of the restless dead. That night, Jed dreamed that his mother stood outside the window and waved at him. She was wearing her old black bathing suit, and much to his relief, had both her breasts. Neither he nor Matty mentioned what they had seen.

Elizabeth dreamed that her dead father was carrying her somewhere, very gently, in his arms.

Chapter III

Some say that Leif Ericksson visited the Island with his Northmen sailors, and that this is the place he called Straumeg, or Island of the Currents. An assemblage of large stones, on a small hill overlooking the up-island pond, may be a cromlech, a Norse burial place. It is certain, however, that Verrazano arrived briefly in 1524, and called the Island "Luisa," beginning the tradition of calling her by a woman's name. In 1602, the first English captain arrived, and gave the place its present, evocative, if slightly mysterious, name. Soon after came the white settlers, the families whose names today mark road signs and stores; they were missionaries and congregationalists, calling themselves the Church of Christ. The Lord's Prayer was translated into the local W. dialect; a literal translation ended with the words: "Always, always wish me so. Amen." Smallpox and Christianity divided the tribes; a remnant *became the Christiantown Indians, who left a small burying ground as their only memorial. The sole surviving community is the Indian town at The Cliffs, the smallest of the Island's five towns. However, in the 1970s the tribe reclaimed the entire town, pointing to old and yet legitimate deeds. Controlling the land and water rights, the tribe began to re-establish its autonomous life.*

Barefoot girls, women in fourteen petticoats, fishermen, farmers, whaling captains with their captains' walks, boats named for women, whale-bone corsets, the flotsam and jetsam of two hundred years and more settled above the tide-line of Island shores. And then, hated and loved, the waves of tourists, potentially as devastating as European to Indian, as rich a hunting ground as the fish-filled sea, arrived on the Island — those scorned out-siders and treasured living – the summer people.

In the mid-1850s, there were great camp meetings at the Bluffs, the largest in the world, in fact, with hymn-singing, hand grasping, prayer, preaching, psalms, shaking, redemption, flirtation, fried chicken, and picnics on the grass. Land boomed, and the feuds began, over water rights, land rights, zoning and conservation, business and recreation, and the Blue Laws that would keep the Island Prohibition-dry.

In Mary's high school yearbook, her quotation had been from Bob Dylan, all about mermaids and Desolation Row.

It might or might not have been a comment on Island life; in any case, her photograph was scowling. Mary had been a brilliant, erratic student, but the high school was so academically poor that with no work at all she was consistently first in her class. An ambitious guidance counselor had gotten her accepted into Harvard; she was the first Islander within recent memory to pass through the gates of the Yard. Once in, she'd felt the critical gaze of the idealized statue of John Harvard; he stared down his aquiline nose at her, a small woman, half Irish, half immigrant mongrel. Surely he had not founded Mother Harvard for the likes of her.

This premonition of exclusion was confirmed on Mary's second day. Hers was the first year that women were admitted as residents of the Yard, where as freshmen they took to beer drinking and panty raiding with an aplomb that shocked their elders. Mary had done none of these things, but had simply washed out her bras and underpants and hung them on the fire escape to dry in the gritty Cambridge sun. She had come equipped with less underwear than her roommates, but that hardly seemed a reason to go dirty. No sooner had she laid out these items than her male proctor appeared, a six-foot blond, who demanded the removal of the unmentionables, and who announced, pronouncing each syllable distinctly, that "this was not a ghet-to."

Mary fulfilled her own prophesy by flunking out midway through her sophomore year. Of course Harvard wished to flunk no one, as they hated to admit the admissions department might have made a mistake, and so they had offered Mary the usual round of summer and make-up courses. By then she was pregnant by her old high school boyfriend. She had an abortion, but took up his gentlemanly offer to marry her. At twenty she was desperate to escape, but the only escape she could conjure was back to the Island. Elizabeth was already a student at Harvard, and the other sisters followed. Harvard liked to take its minorities and geographical distribution by family; of the seven Puerto Ricans in the entire place, three were brothers.

Mary could not adjust to the conversations of Harvard and Harvard Square. All her life she'd listened to Island gossip, the slow but ever-moving tide of news and opinion: tales of the sea, fish runs, clam beds, and boats, disputes over water rights, land rights, and rights of way, wells that were dug and wells that ran dry, pregnancy, childbirth, drunkenness, incest, adultery, battering, wives who ran away and wives who stayed, stories of lingering sickbeds, mysterious illness, premonitions of death, affecting farewells, and disputes over wills, sad and happy opinions of drownings, hurricanes, tourists, Steamship Authority corruption, the decline of the fisheries, acid rain, wood-burning stoves, hit and run accidents, and above and beyond all, the price of land.

Unlike Elizabeth, Mary could never adjust to having chats about South African racism, the clitoral versus the vaginal orgasm, the preppy look. She was uninterested in football, or the history of science, or even in the question of whether it was politically incorrect to sleep with men. So Mary left

33

Harvard and married a taciturn man who liked to talk about cars and fish, and who did not like to talk about making love. She soon found they had nothing to say to each other.

The only professionals Mary acquired in Cambridge were a dentist, a gynecologist, and a hairdresser. In the mythology of her sisters, no professional on the Island could be trusted to cut one's hair or examine one's cervix, and so several times a year Mary went and visited with Therese and pursued her pap smear or layered look. Today, as she boarded the Greyhound bus for Woods Hole, rain streaked the windows with the sad freezing grey of early winter.

Copley Square was grey under the rain and low flat sky. Mary liked the public library, although the hopelessly obscure names on the lintel always amused her: none of the obvious greats for provincial, intellectual Boston. The two churches gracing the Square stood in loose conjunction, surprisingly beautiful inside, with Persian rugs and chandeliers, bright inside despite their drab exteriors, like geodes, those plain-looking rocks that open to reveal glittering quartz or amethyst. All this even though one of the churches, Mary forgot which, was Unitarian.

The bus swung out on to the southeast expressway, a few merciful hours before the rush hour traffic. Mary knew every landmark of the journey from Boston to the Cape by heart, but her favorite was the great oil tank that sat on the bayside. On it, Corita, the abstract expressionist painter who was also a nun, had painted gigantic flowing streams of color: red, blue, yellow, green. And if you looked carefully — as Mary and her sisters invariably did — you could see the profile of Ho Chi Minh in the great blue streak: eyebrows, nose, and especially wispy beard, looking out over Boston and seeming to promise the stern tropical paradise of revolution.

The night Saigon fell, Mary had been visiting Therese in her dorm on the Radcliffe campus. That was the year that Therese, in her all-women dorm by choice, had become a conscious lesbian; and Mary, a married woman visiting the campus, felt awkward and strange. But for a moment, in the cool violet spring air, when the news came, the sisters had been for a moment in perfect accord, and hung out the old Viet Cong flag, veteran of so many demonstrations. The single star shone in the dusk, and later there had been a bit of minor revelry in the Square, but they hadn't gone, because Therese said it was just some crazy left-wing splinter groups. Mary was glad she was with Therese instead of Joe, because Joe would have been enraged by her sympathies. He'd had a first cousin killed in the war, and would have stood for the draft himself except that he was six months too young for the final call. But those images of that exquisite, desolate country remained imprinted in Mary's mind's eye, of refugees on the road fleeing from the fiery air; and even after stories of the atrocities came out, and refugees began to fill Boston, she retained an inviolable image of Vietnam as something delicate and precious she was ashamed to have broken.

Mary was depressed. She watched the raindrops flatten against the window of the bus; she watched the exit signs say "Duxbury" and "Plymouth" like something out of a history book; she ate an entire package of M & M s with peanuts, and she felt no better. Her life was a mess, a waste, a confusion. She was almost thirty and had done nothing at all. Her marriage was a failure. This in itself brought a peculiar kind of relief, as life with Joe had become increasingly claustrophobic. She was practically a virgin, having slept only with her husband and with only one short fling and a sole one night stand during a duller course of her marriage.

She'd had a dozen years of mundane, underpaid jobs, most of them seasonal tourist trade: waitress, pastry chef, caterer, housecleaner, caretaker, babysitter. She had a high school diploma and a shack that sat on a three-acre site that was now worth close to half a million dollars. She had inherited the land from her father, and as she did not mean to traffic in real estate — her mother's current palliative for depression — she was reduced to living in the shack and working at shit jobs.

She was depressed, she was ten pounds overweight, she had no prospects, no lover, no baby, no career. And worst of all, she felt that even if she had these things, terror would still pursue her. "I'm going to die," she said to herself so loudly that she feared she had spoken aloud, but no one on the bus noticed. She was going to die, if not immediately then inevitably, and if not in some hideous nuclear destruction of the whole planet then in some hideous personal destruction, like her mother's friend Muriel, of cancer or just simply as a senile old lady.

Mary had a backpack full of books with the word "Zen" in their titles. She'd bought every one she could find in the Cambridge bookstores. Also books with the title "woman" or "alone," purporting to be about female solitude, although the dust jacket photographs showed the authors cuddling their cats, so invariably they weren't quite alone. Mary also had a quarter of a gram of coke wrapped up neatly in silver foil, courtesy of her almost ex-husband Joe, who dealt a little coke on the side. Elizabeth told Mary she needed therapy; Therese said she should move to Cambridge and join a woman's group; Cathy thought she should go back to college and have a career. At the moment, she relied on the books and the cocaine.

The bus stopped at Buzzard's Bay before the canal: rain over the sad bundled people, the hardware store and gas stations lit up like Christmas trees, the streets shutting down under winter. The sight of the bridge lifted her spirits for a moment, but then she wondered what she had to look forward to. Home. There was no home. Nothing was ever going to happen to her again.

At Falmouth, even in the rain, the old dignified houses looked beautiful, grey, austere. The last leaves were slick and wet on the grand trees. In the window of one lighted house a child played the piano. Outside the town hall, a statue of a Revolutionary War soldier stood still in the yellow leaves and rain. The wind buffeted the bus from side to side. Coming down into Wood's Hole the sea looked frighteningly choppy. Mary was glad she wasn't out in it, and then realized that of course she still had to take the ferry home.

A few disgruntled passengers sat in the harshly lit over-heated office of the Steamship Authority. All but one of the ticket windows was closed. The rain was really coming down now, slanting at an angle. The barometer on the wall showed pressure falling. Peering out of a steamy window, Mary saw that no ferry was in sight. Both of the slips were bare.

To calm herself, and also because her bladder was uncomfortably full after the bus ride, she went to the ladies' room and pissed in the glare of the chlorine-colored light. She liked the ladies' room of the Steamship Authority, a familiar way station, a ritual cleansing place. As she sat on the toilet she read the usual graffiti and a bold new addition that read:

REAL WOMEN DON'T EAT MEN. She laughed, and felt in her bag for her own writing implement, a blunted stick of old bright red lipstick. Mary took the lipstick and then, hesitating as to what to write, the cover of one of her new Zen books served an inspiration. In sticky red she drew a circle, almost a complete circle but one that suddenly opened up, incomplete and yet dynamic. After happily regarding her handiwork she got up and scrubbed her hands with the harsh soap. In the green mirror she looked hellish, and she was glad to return to the land of the living, outside again.

But the Steamship Authority gave her no satisfaction. "Is there a five fifteen ferry?" she asked the teenaged clerk. As it was already 5:10 P.M. her question really meant: so where is the ferry? The kid scowled at her.

"Hurricane warning," he said.

"Is there going to be another ferry tonight?"

He gestured helplessly around the waiting room. "I wouldn't count on it."

"Yes or no?" She was outraged, and a little panicky.

"Look, lady, it's not my fault," he said. "We'll know for sure in an hour or two."

Mary backed off helplessly. She hated being called "lady." Then she heard a tentative voice call her by her proper name: "Mary?" She turned and saw a tall young man, conventionally dressed in a salt-and-pepper suit, with an incongruous pair of vivid yellow rain boots, holding out his hand to her. For an awful moment, she had no idea who he was; then she recognized her sister Cathy's fiance, John the banker, whom she had met on two previous occasions.

Therese, in a fit of nastiness, had noticed the dull names of her sisters' men: Joe, Jed, John. Not only were the names hopelessly boring, but they all began with the letter J. She took to referring to them indiscriminately as the "Big J." Of course Therese's Lu had an equally mundane and ridiculous name, but the phrase "Big J" echoed in Mary's mind, and she was afraid she would blurt it out to John.

Instead, she formally shook his hand, suddenly self-conscious about her appearance: her ratty jeans, her ancient down jacket. "Hello," she said. His warm, firm hand made her suddenly very glad to see him, although she simultaneously despised herself for still harboring fantasies of rescue by knights in shining armour or in banker's suits.

"It doesn't look as if there'll be a ferry out tonight."

"Oh, you don't think so? They said maybe there would be. There's still the possibility, they said."

"No, the wind is rising, there's been small craft warnings out since afternoon, and I'm sure the hurricane is about to hit."

"What am I going to do? I can't get home," she said, suddenly helpless, but hating herself for whining.

"Have you had dinner?"

"No." She was ravenous.

"You know Woods Hole better than I do, Mary. Can you suggest a good place to eat?" His manner of speaking was stilted and formal, but not unpleasant.

"Yes," she said. "Let's go to the Black Cat Cafe. It's excellent, and just around the corner."

She could hear the rain pouring down and the docks creaking. Mary wished suddenly that she was nailed down, like a roof or a boat. John's clean-cut, polite demeanor reminded her of certain boys in high school, boys she would have scorned to know when she'd been Hippie Queen, but she was obscurely grateful. She was afraid of the storm.

They dashed out into the rain, but by the time they made the door of the dockside cafe, they were thoroughly soaked. Mary felt her sneakers slosh and thought of pneumonia.

The Black Cat was foggy with steam, and smelled of clam chowder, fried potatoes, and espresso. They both ordered chowder and hamburgers.

"You're not a vegetarian?" John asked.

"Why, did Cathy tell you I was the hippie of the family?"

"Well . . . " she almost thought she saw him blush. So, he was shy, that was to his credit. But now what? Should she ask him about his job? His family? It was all too boring. She ate a gigantic homefry instead.

But John had turned the rather gentle force of his attention on her.

"What are your plans? Cathy said you might be moving to Boston."

"Yes, I'm planning to . . . particularly if this weather keeps up!" She surprised herself. Since when had she decided that?

38

"It must be pretty dismal on the Island this time of the year."

"Oh, it can be beautiful, too," she said defensively.

"By the way, Cathy told me about you and Joe. I just wanted to say I'm sorry, and that I hope things work out for you. Your sister is worried about you, but I told her not to be, because you were a beautiful foxy woman with a great future ahead of you."

She felt a hot tear in the corner of her eye. No one in her family had spoken to her so gently on the subject.

"Thank you," she said softly. And then recovering herself a bit harshly, added, "I suppose that the last thing an engaged couple wants to hear about is a divorce."

"Well, my parents were divorced when I was quite young. My father left my mother, you know, just ran out on her, and she supported us. She's a trained EMT and drove an ambulance until she retired. We were raised more by my grandmother. Two very tough ladies. Very tough. Driving an ambulance is grueling work; you see all kinds of things." He sounded proud.

"I'm not sure where you're from, where you grew up."

"Queens. You know, New York. Flushing, Queens." His perfect banker's accent creaked a little as he named his hometown. Mary liked him more for having been poor, for being fatherless; it added a gleam of charm to his almost standardized tall blondness.

"You know," he continued, "I love your sister so much. She's so warm and understanding. But she's tough too. And first in her work. Even though my parents were divorced, I think your sister and I can make a go of things. I have faith. She opened my heart. I was such a cynic. Not that I think you don't have to work at a marriage. But I think we can do it." As if embarrassed by his sentiment, he hurriedly picked up the check. "It's on me," he said, hurrying to the cash register. Mary noted with the satisfaction of an ex-waitress that he overtipped.

Back at the Steamship Authority they were greeted by a locked door and a penciled sign: NO FERRY TONIGHT. CHECK FOR 5:45 A.M. SAT. Mary and John looked at each other. The odd romance of the situation made them uneasy.

"We should get a motel," he said, trying to sound casual.

39

"I can't afford it." She felt blank. If she'd been alone she would have slept in her jacket on the porch of the office or looked up an acquaintance in Woods Hole. Or maybe even gone back to Boston.

"Don't worry. I've got plenty of plastic. Do you know of any place that's good?"

She laughed. She'd never had a reason to go into a motel in Woods Hole in her life. "The closer the better," she said, pointing through the rainy gloom at a red neon sign: SAL'S MOTEL and VACANCIES. Woods Hole was just a little dump, with everything piled up near the ferry: motels, cafes, liquor stores, all the small necessities of transit. Often the place had bored Mary; how many idle hours had she spent there, watching the seals at the aquarium or drinking beer and trying to avoid getting tan lines from her T-shirt. But now she was glad everything was close together.

They dashed into the lobby of Sal's. The matron behind the desk, Sal no doubt, squinted at them out of suspicious Cape Cod eyes, but she took John's MasterCard without a question. Mary's clothes were dripping, forming a small pool on the kelly green indoor-outdoor carpeting. The room Sal showed them was "just fine, thank you," with a big double bed and an almost equally large color TV set. Mary noted with disappointment that there was no Magic Fingers vibrator for the bed. She'd only been in a motel once before, with Joe when she was in college, and they had spent much of the time feeding quarters into the Magic Fingers.

"Maybe we should get a cot," said John, looking suddenly chaste in his pink and white coloring.

"Oh, don't bother. We're practically related," said Mary. She was lonely now.

"You can take the first shower. I want to call Cathy, anyway. She's up-island at your mother's, probably worrying right this minute about where I am." He pulled out another charge card.

Mary went into the shining bathroom, ran steaming water into the tub, and left her clothes in a wet pile. Then, for once thinking practically, she washed out everything, including her mud-stained sneakers, and set them out to dry by the old-fashioned radiator. Then she sank into the tub. The water was blissfully hot — wasn't that her mother's word, blissful? That and "delicious;" Matty never offered anyone a piece of fruit without the preface "delicious." "Here, have a delicious apple, a delicious pear." The daughters teased her for it, but maybe Matty was right, maybe things really were delicious. Matty had been so poor; for her, running that supermarket must have been almost a luxury rather than just the necessity of making a living. All that fruit! All those vegetables! Mary had once seen her mother, while arranging the vegetables, pick up a bunch of leeks and hold them to her face as if she wanted to inhale them. "Kissing vegetables?" teased Mary, old enough to know what Freudian was. But Matty had just smiled vaguely. Why was she thinking of that now? God! It must have been ten years ago. Anyway, the hot water was delicious. And how amazing, it just came out of the tap, no problem at all. Everything was going to be just fine if there was no nuclear war. She wouldn't want to be on an island during a nuclear war: too lingering a death, and having to see everybody from high school. Better to go to Boston where at least she could get killed instantly. Elizabeth said that thinking a lot about death meant that you were depressed, but Mary thought she was just being realistic.

She ran some more hot water, turning on the tap with her foot. She looked at her foot. It was a nice foot, small, almost translucently white. Her stomach was fat, disgusting, a hideous bulge. Her pubic hair was blonde, a great advantage in this world, and her breasts were, dare she say it, yes, perfect: medium-sized melons, firm, long-nippled. This quick body scan gave her a yearning to see her face. Luckily she had borrowed one of Elizabeth's nightgowns; she could look presentable and not traumatize John. The nightgown was a little short, but otherwise fit perfectly, even if Elizabeth weighed at least seven pounds less than she did. In the mirror she saw her pale worried face, her too-small greenish blue eyes wrinkled by squinting, her shoulder-length blonde hair that made her visible, a shining beacon in the street, something desirable, although a bit cliched. And blondes were supposed to age early. Maybe she should lighten her hair? She peered at herself. Except for the squint lines, she looked about eleven years old, especially in the white batiste nightgown.

Luckily for John, she didn't want to frighten him. If she had been Elizabeth she would have seduced him, if she had been Therese she would have insisted on the cot, and if she had been Cathy, she would have wanted to marry him. But she wasn't any of them, she was herself, no matter how sad, how ill-defined she felt, and she pushed her hair behind her ears in an old self-reassuring gesture, even though her sisters said it made her look severe. Then she stuck out her tongue at herself and crossed her eyes. This always cheered her up, and gave her the courage to leave the womb of the bathroom.

John smiled at her when she came out. "Cathy sends you her love," he said. He seemed grateful for the shower, and for the fact that she was already in bed when he came back, and disinclined to make conversation. Neither of them burdened the other with sleepy confidences or words beyond a simple "good night." The situation was too delicate, Mary thought, and a cozy talk might lead too easily into cozy sex. Besides, she was glad to be alone with her thoughts. It had been an odd day, a day of transit, and now sleep was her only destination.

So she slept, and toward morning when the storm lightened and the sky finally cleared Mary dreamed she saw her husband Joe standing at the bottom of her bed. He was dripping wet, and covered with seaweed, and by these signs she knew that he had drowned. He looked at her reproachfully, as if she rather than he was somehow at fault in their relationship, and then he turned away.

The dream was so powerful that when Mary returned to the Island she half expected to hear news of his death. But instead she ran into him at the supermarket, and they exchanged some hostile pleasantries.

When John got off the ferry the next morning, Cathy ran up to him and threw her arms around him. Mary knew she had to do something. "I have to concentrate," she said to herself.

Chapter IV

At present, the Island lies as always, touched by two kinds of tides: the tide of sea, low and high, summer and winter, sun and moon, and the tide of people: the summer people from New York and Boston, professionals, artists, intellectuals, preppies, middle-class Blacks and Jews, from those who own land to the scorned day-trippers; and the year-round people: fishermen, carpenters, weavers, librarians, high school kids and hoods, poor farmers made rich by real estate, Indians, urban escapees, hippies who stayed, — but no first or even second generation is considered to be a true Islander. In winter, they subsist on food stamps or trust funds, alcohol, cottage industry, caretaking jobs, or follow the tourist trade south to Florida and the Keys; and then in summer the flood returns again, the tanned girls in their turquoise bikinis, the burnt boys in pick-up trucks, green leaves, wild flowers, vegetable gardens, and the clear warm waves.

"I've found the perfect place," said Therese. Mary looked at her blankly. Was Therese trying to get rid of her already?

"Perfect?"

"Perfect. It's in Cambridgeport . . ."

"A shitty neighborhood, too close to the river, full of junkies and murderers."

"Very central, though. Near the women's center and the co-op. You can bike everywhere.

"Very dangerous. I'll probably get mugged and raped and killed."

"But the house itself is just fantastic, six huge bedrooms, five feminists looking for a sixth . . ."

"Lesbian."

"Calm down, Mary," snapped Therese. "They aren't all lesbians. And the house is gigantic and . . ."

"Costs an arm and a leg to heat."

"Heat is included by the landlord. I asked. You're lucky to have me looking out for you. This is a real find. Why, there's a backyard and a basement with a ping pong table, and besides, the place is famous. They give really great parties at Owl House."

"Owl House?"

"Yes! It even has a name, this house. Owl House because there is an owl carved over the fireplace, which has become the totem of the house. Over the years everyone has collected lots of owl figures and put them up everywhere. Lu says it's particularly appropriate because the owl is the symbol of the goddess Athena, virgin goddess of wisdom."

"Are these virgins?"

"Cut it out."

"Does the fireplace work?"

"Unfortunately, no."

"Pet owls?"

"No, pet cats, three of them. All male."

"Oh."

"Oh?"

"I'll move in," said Mary grudgingly. "When is it available?"

"Tomorrow, so you'd better step on it; and they want first and last month's rent. I hope you can come up with it."

"Yes," said Mary, although that meant the last of her savings. "I guess I'll have to start looking for a job."

Therese felt light with relief. Her sister had been camping out on her living room couch, alternating between despair and snappishness, with an occasional ray of charming goodwill that she usually turned on not at Therese but at Lu.

"I like your sister. She's having a hard time but she's a strong woman," said Lu.

"She's just a pain in the ass, as far as I'm concerned. What is she moping about?"

"Well, she just separated from her husband."

"Tough." Therese looked scornful. "He was one unmitigated asshole. It's just as well. Besides, marriage is an oppressive patriarchal institution. She's better off on her own."

"I was married once, too, you know."

"I know you were, sweetie," said Therese, and put her arms around Lu. Lu was so much smaller than she that the top of her head came just up to Therese's chin. But somehow this made both of them feel secure. "I'm glad you don't live in Berkeley, or have a white male oppressor husband any more," said Therese.

"You're white," Lu pointed out.

"Yes, yes, and an oppressor," said Therese, laughing with her.

Yet for all her complaints, Therese felt Mary to be her responsibility. After all, who else in the family had anything real to offer a newly divorced young woman? She, Therese, could get Mary to move back to Cambridge, get her involved in the women's movement, get her to meet people, even fall in love again, but this time more appropriately, and turn her life around.

It was odd that Mary's younger sisters were always in the position of rescuing her; not that she ever asked for help, but her helplessness made them feel strong. Even Elizabeth and Therese were now on temporarily cordial terms because of

45

Mary. They enjoyed long telephone conferences wherein they speculated about her possibilities, crudely evaluated her chances for love and sex on the open Cambridge market, and could not restrain themselves from self-congratulation as to how much better they had turned out than she.

While Therese found Mary a house, Elizabeth now found her a job.

"Cocktail waitressing? Where?"

"At Rick's Cafe. It's in the Square. Lots of rattan. Fake ceiling fans. You know the place, right off the alley. It's full of preppies."

"I don't have any experience."

"I lied and said you did. A friend of mine just quit and I got you the job. And why worry about it. You've done lots of waitressing, after all."

"Yes, but that was at those family fish places on the Island. I'm sure this is totally different, complicated drink orders and all."

"Better tips. Cute guys."

"From Harvard. Assholes who think you're a piece of meat just because you're a waitress."

"You went to Harvard, too."

"Barely."

"But think of the good hours. Your days are free. That'll be nice. We can do things together because I'm only teaching three days a week."

"But my nights will be full of drunks and townies."

"You can't object to both Harvard and townies at the same time. Make up your mind!"

"I'll be exhausted from running away from all those men."

"The bartender will protect you if you want him to."

"I have nothing to wear."

"I'll lend you something."

"Oh, thank you, Elizabeth, you're a darling, just a darling. I'm not worth it. Everyone is being so nice to me and I just don't deserve it, I'm just a useless slob, but thank you anyway."

Elizabeth kissed her, melting with sympathy just as she was about to regret the loan of her clothes. Her clothes never quite fit Mary anyway, who was a little bigger than she. Then again, her black silky skirt was long and just might do. She had a bunch of black tops, camisoles almost, that were too slinky for teaching. Elizabeth had acquired them in her early graduate school days when she was a teaching fellow by day and whorish by night, but therapy and Howard and then Jed had put an end to her cruising, and she was ready to pass on the lace and satin numbers. Usually Elizabeth's clothes were all the wrong colors for Mary, who was as fair as Elizabeth was dark, but they both looked good in black.

Mary was incorrigible at the moment, thought Elizabeth, but at least she was being nice to Jed, and in a genuine non-flirtatious way.

"I like your sister," said Jed. Mary had practically come along as a third when he and Elizabeth moved in together.

"She's a pain in the ass."

"She'll get better once she gets over the divorce. Anyway, she's pretty and sad and smart and I'm sure the guys will be crawling all over her. It's an irresistible combination."

"Am I?"

"Irresistible?"

"Irresistible, pretty, and sad."

"Definitely pretty and irresistible, but not sad."

"Would I be more irresistible sad?" Elizabeth pouted in a way she knew was irresistible.

"You're perfect," he said, and kissed her. "And besides, how can you be sad when you have me, not to mention this gorgeous apartment?"

"We have no furniture," she pointed out.

"But we have a bed," he said, "so why don't you come over here if you're sad?" So she did.

Mary moved into Owl House first and examined it later. It was not quite perfect, being old and frayed around the edges, with great dusty carpets and mouldering woodwork that no amount of cleaning could actually get clean, but Mary's room was pleasant enough, with a high ceiling and a warm southern exposure. Her first night there she felt odd, unfamiliar even to herself, as if when she went to sleep in the old mahogany bed that came with the room and on the sheets she had borrowed from Elizabeth she would wake up in a different life. But in the morning she seemed to have re-entered herself again, no Sleeping Beauty awakened by a kiss or butterfly emerging from a cocoon, just Mary, looking sleepily at her own hands and feet for reassurance and finding herself the same.

In Owl House there were four, not three, cats, and the fourth was an expectant mother. All three stories of the house were strewn with cat hair. One had only to sit down anywhere in a pair of black pants to become painfully aware of this fact. The phone rang constantly, the bathroom was always occupied, and the five roommates dashed about, running from work to political meetings to love affairs, to the movies, leaving each other elaborate messages in crayon tacked to the refrigerator. They seemed pleasant enough, and kept the two refrigerators filled with vegetables and cheese and co-op cider, but no one made any particular effort to be Mary's friend. She felt rather dazed by their comings and goings. Life on the Island had certainly been more lethargic, but she was grateful for anonymity for the first time in her life. No one noticed if she slept till noon or took a two-hour bath by candlelight in the middle of the day. She grew partial to the view out her window, the low landscape of old houses and decrepit gardens, and a bare tree, lovely and grey, pointing skyward like a candelabra just beyond the glass.

Her sisters, however, were determined not to leave her in her new-found peace. It was true that she did have a fair amount of free time. She worked only four nights a week at the bar, and to her surprise the work was both slow-paced and lucrative. It did take Mary a few days to adjust her level of flirtation to the new situation. At the family fish restaurants on the Island she had always flirted her ass off with each fat tourist paterfamilias, for they tipped lavishly on their credit cards and were restrained from more than leering at her by the presence of their polyester-clad wives. But at the bar, flirtation led too easily into attempted seduction, and did not seem to affect the tips, which were steady from the regulars and unpredictable from the transients. And as for seduction, attempted or consummated, she was just not up to it with the young men whose hairy wrists protruded from tweedy jackets as they held their glasses of dark beer or shots of tequila and vodka.

Even if she had not slept until noon, Mary had much of the day free, not to mention the unemployed portion of the beginning of the week, a desert of time that could not be filled even with a library card, making soup, attempting to read a book with Zen ox-herding pictures, washing her panty hose, mending her bras, and morbidly fantasizing about the past and the future, a technique which unsuccessfully tried to keep the present firmly in check.

Her sisters took her in hand.

"I've signed you up for the Tuesday night group at the women's center," said Therese, who was calling during an afternoon lull at work.

"You've what?"

"Mary, it's for your own good. You need to meet people."

"I don't want to meet people, I'm surrounded by people all day long."

Elizabeth took a different track. Although she would have liked to have gotten Mary into therapy with someone good, she saw the hopelessness of this cause. So instead she settled on trying to provide Mary with company, amusement, and perhaps more contact with the finer things of the intellect: art and music. Since Elizabeth herself hated classical music, this left art. As for company, this would be provided by Elizabeth, whose calming artistic influence could not be underrated.

"Your sister is on the phone!" yelled one of the Owl House roommates.

"Which one?" Mary yelled back. "Tell whoever it is that I'm not home."

"It's Elizabeth!" yelled the roommate.

Mary picked up the phone. "How are you?" asked Elizabeth.

"Oh, fine. Horrible," said Mary.

"Let's have lunch and go to the museum," said Elizabeth, pitching her voice into its most winning register.

"Oh . . ." Mary could not claim to hate the Boston Museum of Fine Arts. She loved the MFA. She even loved Elizabeth. She just didn't want to bother. Then she panicked that she was losing the will to live. "Okay," she mumbled. "When?"

"Today. I'll meet you at the Central Square T at 11 o'clock," said Elizabeth, slamming down the phone before Mary could protest.

At the museum Mary followed Elizabeth. She wasn't quite at home with the remodeled new space, not that the old MFA had been any less confusing, with its series of circular corridors that seemed inevitably to lead to the Huntington Avenue exit and never to the Impressionist paintings.

"What is your favorite?" asked Mary. It was an old game between them, what's your favorite ice cream flavor, season, book, other sister, presidential candidate, sexual position.

"My favorite? Of anything in the museum? Whole museum?"

"Uh huh."

"Well then, I'll show you," said Elizabeth, and led her sister a few galleries deeper into the painting collection. "Here." She stopped in front of a John Singer Sargent painting showing four girls, wide eyed, in sailor dresses with their long blonde hair pulled back too tightly in subdued ribbons. The little girls faced forward, accompanied or surrounded by enormous Oriental vases that were as big as they were. The tallest girl stool slightly behind the others, her face obscured in shadow.

"Oh . . ." said Mary, "it's us." Elizabeth gave her a rare smile of complete approval. She thought she'd have to explain why it was her favorite, Sargent because he was American, from the gloomy previous century, looking like a Henry James novel, and sad, because someone valued their possessions as much as the little girls. The painting seemed to have the whole New England story in it. However, Mary might not have cared to understand all this intellectualizing, and besides, the real reason that Elizabeth loved the painting was just what Mary had picked up on; somehow the little now long dead girls in their sailor dresses felt like Elizabeth and her sisters.

They stood in quiet contemplation before the painting, poised together in a friendly silence. Then Elizabeth countered: "Your favorite?"

"Oh, Watson and the Shark." After watching the girls, Mary felt the need to be flip.

Elizabeth groaned. Watson and the Shark showed someone named Mr. Watson who had tumbled, apparently quite naked, into a colonial Boston Harbor, which was still clean enough to house sharks, one of which was now trying to eat Mr. Watson, whose companions in a small, desperately overcrowded rowboat were attempting to save him by posing as a Revolutionary War statue and looking heavenward. Was it possible that Mary was identifying herself as the hapless Mr. Watson, the hysterical rescuers with her sisters, and the shark with the threatening forces in her life, perhaps even soon to be ex-husband Joe? In any case, this could not be considered anyone's officially favorite painting, any more than "Jaws" could be considered anyone's favorite movie, even if all your friends were extras in it because it was filmed on the Island.

"Forget it, it doesn't count," said Elizabeth, as they began to stroll through the Impressionists: Renoir's bright dancing couple, Mrs. Monet in a peculiar kimono, and Manet's guitar player stepping out into the street with her blank and wistful face. The museum smelled warm and familiar, one of the few places that was still overheated despite oil prices; and the flutter of perfumed matrons seemed more decorative than intimidating for once. Turning the corner, Mary saw Gauguin's large triptych.

"That's it, my favorite," she said.

" 'Where did we come from? Where are we now? Where are we going?' " translated Elizabeth from the French.

"Good question," Mary murmured to herself. They looked at the brilliant bold figures, a woman with a child, a dog, an idol with outstretched arms, sensuous young girls, an old bent woman. Elizabeth suspected that Mary just liked it because although colorful it was ultimately depressing. Where are we going? Why, towards the old bent woman, none too cheerful an idea, particularly for Elizabeth at that moment, who was in love and felt life opening out before her.

Mary liked the painting because she couldn't understand it, and it tormented her in a way. The figures seemed to describe the question more than answer it, yet it was a question that she was desperate to answer. Still, the bodies of the women were beautiful.

"It's nice, one of his best," said Elizabeth politely, and Mary did not ask for more of a response.

Elizabeth had to look at some furnishings in the American wing as background for a class she was teaching. After the questions, Mary felt the urge to be alone, and so they agreed to meet for lunch in half an hour.

Mary wandered off towards the Oriental collection. This part of the museum was almost deserted, of dark wood and smelling mustier than the newer parts. Mary had some vague idea of a rock garden with sand raked into waves and swirls, but she wasn't sure where to find it. She ambled along, stopping to admire a small green glaze vase, a row of dazzling Kabuki kimonos, a calligraphic scroll hidden under a brocade covering. She turned a corner and found herself in an unfamiliar part of the museum, a dead end which seemed to lead into some sort of reconstructed temple. The gate to the temple was shut, with a sign "By Permission Only," but no one was about and the gate wasn't really locked, only latched, so she let herself in. Years of trespassing on Island beaches, of crossing other people's land to swim or surf or fish, had made Mary bold, and a disbeliever in too much private property.

Inside the gate, it was dark and smelled faintly of sandalwood or some other kind of incense. In the gloom Mary could make out a series of large statues of Buddhas and other figures. Moved by some impulse, she sat down cross-legged on the cold floorboards and looked at the altar. On either side stood grim figures brandishing swords, one in each of their many hands. They scowled, but did not seem to direct their wrath at her. So she sat quietly, looking at the central Buddha, who was carved in wood and covered in gilt that was peeling off with age. The Buddha statue appeared to look back at her, serene, remote, but kind, with that faint smile or half-smile flickering about the lips. The Buddha was sitting in the middle of a golden flower. Mary wished she knew the story about who the Buddha was, and what country the statue was from, but mostly she wanted to understand the Buddha's expression, a look of quiet and not-quiet, of stillness and not-stillness, of motion and not-motion.

"Excuse me, ma'am," said a voice with the harshest of Boston accents. It was one of the MFA guards, not looking as wrathful as the guardian deities, but still unpleasant. "This is closed. Can't you read?"

"Sorry," said Mary, adjusting her posture and getting up.

"Open by appointment only," he reiterated crossly.

"I'm sorry," she snapped. But she wasn't sorry in the least.

Still, she did not mention the incident to Elizabeth. At lunch, over the attempted chic soup and salad of the museum restaurant, the urge to gossip became overwhelming.

"I guess Cathy is going to marry that guy," said Elizabeth, with faint enthusiasm.

"John? Yes, I think so. You know, he's actually nice, not nearly as stiff as he seems at first."

"That's right, you were in a motel room with him the night of the storm. Does he look cute in pajamas? Did you get it on with him?"

"Elizabeth! Don't be disgusting!" They both laughed. "I thought you liked him! Anyway, do you think it's a good idea for Cathy to marry him? You know, she still seems like a baby to me, unformed. Is she really set on that banking? It seems like an awfully dull life to me."

"Well, she's not like us." They sat together in happy collusion, although it was an odd fact that when any two of the sisters were together they felt "like us," the others haplessly excluded, maligned, misunderstood.

It was true, however, that Cathy was the baby of the family, the caboose, and that she was more removed from the sometimes hysterical dynamic of her three older sisters. For now, as the Thanksgiving holidays approached, Therese and Elizabeth began to lose interest in their mission to rescue Mary. Elizabeth felt the trip to the museum had been a success, and Therese was content when Mary agreed to go to the Tuesday evening group at the women's center. They also withdrew from Mary in large part because she seemed increasingly cheerful but no more increasingly grateful. Cathy, however, more removed, but still guiltily aware of Mary's divorce and sufferings, stepped into the breach, bearing what she considered to be a woman's mainstay of mental health: clothes.

So Cathy called Matty on the phone: "Ma, Mary's depressed, so why don't you give us the charge cards and I'll take her clothes shopping?" Matty readily agreed, out of similar faint guilt and powerful belief in the antidotal quality of a new sweater.

"I'm taking you shopping," announced Cathy, in the ubiquitous abrupt phone manner of the family. "And don't try to get out of it," she continued, as Mary made small noises of panic. It was pouring sleet the early evening they planned to meet outside of Hyacinth, one of Cambridge's chic boutiques. Even Cathy felt bedraggled, as if the quick walk from the

T station had turned her from business professional into drowned waif. Her too-thin boots were wrong for the unseasonable weather. As she trudged along the icy sidewalk, she was struck suddenly with the finality of her life. Would she marry John? Yes. And live with him forever and never so much as sleep with another man, limiting her infidelity to party flirtations? Most probably. But somehow the knowledge of all of this felt like a blow to the solar plexus. No more riding around on the back of motorcycles with hoody types who were beneath her, no more emotionally empty but nonetheless fascinating sex with colleagues who were attracted by her combination of competence and sexiness. Was she too young? John was officially moving in this weekend, giving up his old lease, and coming to live with her. She liked him, she loved him, she tamped down the panic inside; surely she, the tamest of the sisters, could learn? But tame as she was, she shared with them a narrow but fierce recklessness. She considered herself to be her sole owner and proprietor.

Mary stood just inside Hyacinth, which looked warm and bright from the street. The shop was painted in an electric blue. At that hour before closing, no saleswoman clad in brilliant stockings and a little black dress assaulted them, so they had the leisure of the racks to themselves. Mary was looking hopefully at the bins of underpants and colorful balls of socks, piled up like greengrocer's wares, but Cathy was not interested in such items. "This . . . and this . . . and this . . . and don't complain," she said, pulling things down. Cathy enjoyed bossing Mary about; it was a new and pleasant experience. Mary squinted at herself in the greenish dressing room mirror. There was a hole in her bra, and one nipple threatened to poke through. Her underpants were a hundred years old, and a peculiar shade of grey. She was a mess. But she had to agree that the clothes that Cathy picked out improved her. They were simple but definite, warm, and they matched: a black wool skirt, a bright red turtleneck sweater of silk and wool.

"I can't wear red," she protested, but she could, it made her look blonder. "Can't I get it in black?" she begged.

"No, but you can try this," said Cathy, handing her a beautiful blue knit dress with odd ivory buttons. It made Mary's eyes look blue.

"Can't I try this in black?"

"No," said Cathy, bundling it all up and taking it to the saleswoman, who glared at her as if she were an orphan drug addict who had stolen the charge cards, and rang the order up anyway.

"Thank you, you've been a darling," said Mary, kissing Cathy. They smiled at each other for the first time that day. "Really, I'm grateful you didn't let me buy all black." Cathy was happy. She'd done something she knew how to do, and for once it had actually affected one of her sisters. "And don't wear these new clothes with some ugly old cast-off," was her parting instruction.

On her way to the meeting at the women's center, Mary wore the new red sweater with a pair of ancient but honorable blue jeans. She added the silver filigreed earrings that Joe had bought her one high school summer in an uncharacteristic fit of romance. Strange, thought Mary, but she did not look half bad. Maybe she was cheering up. This possibility made her scowl.

The women's center was in a dangerous and poverty-stricken part of town, down by the river, just a few blocks from Owl House. Mary walked rapidly, her keys clenched in her fist, one between each finger, ready to defend herself. Therese had taught her this technique, as well as giving her a whistle. Fear made Mary short-breathed, and she would rather rely on a scream. Still, nothing happened, and she arrived safely.

The women's center was an old large house with a sagging porch and dirt patch garden. The rooms in its sprawling three stories were outfitted with old couches, multicolored pillows, and political posters like the ones in Therese's apartment. There was also a black cat named Emma, for Emma Goldman. Mary was late, and when she found the meeting room, six women looked appraisingly up at her. "Sit down," someone said, offering her a cushion. "We're just about to introduce ourselves and begin."

Mary looked around, wondering who would be kind, who would be a friend.

"Let me introduce myself," said a thin pretty woman,with dark hair pulled back off her face. Mary noticed her long delicate hands and feet, her slightly bumpy nose, her deep eyes. Did she look a little bit like Matty's friend Muriel? The woman continued, in a nasal New York accent, "My name is Jessica, I'm from New York originally, but I've lived in Boston for eight years. I've been part of the women's center for four, and I'm here to facilitate, help get the group going. I'm not really a leader, I'm part of the group, too. I live by myself, I'm a mental health worker, and I'm glad to be here, although nervous because it's the first time. Oh, I forgot to mention, I actually live with my cat!" Everyone laughed, even Mary. Jessica seemed so self assured but also a bit breezy; Mary envied her. And she liked watching Jessica's hands.

Jessica turned almost imperceptibly to the woman on her left, who after a long silent moment introduced herself. She was a tall, muscular woman, with a broad face and grey eyes. Her hair was short and she wore a heavy ring dangling with keys on her belt."Hi," she said. "I'm Alice. I've lived in Boston for a long time but I'm originally from outside Chicago. I have an unpronounceable Polish last name . . ." Everyone laughed. "I work on the railroad, trained through CETA. I work with men all day so I wanted to spend an evening with women . . . I'm nervous, too, because because I'm looking around this room wondering if anyone else here is a lesbian."

Two women waved at her, but Jessica said, "Let's go around in order." Mary was counting frantically to herself: Alice, plus the two wavers, plus who knew what Jessica was. She looked exotic, probably bisexual or something. This left only three straight women. She felt outnumbered. Damn Therese; it was all her fault.

The next woman started in with a headlong dash: "Tish. I was born in Cambridge . . ." She had delicate cheek bones and was very blonde. "I'm from a WASP family, my father teaches at Harvard." She looked embarrassed, but relieved to be confessing. "I work for the women's center, writing grant proposals, but I work alone so I don't see many women over the course of the day. Oh, I'm a hand-raising lesbian. I don't really feel comfortable here tonight, but I hope I'll learn to." Mary liked her face; she felt honest, if skittish.

The woman next to her said: "I'm the other lesbian! My name is Sandy. I'm a lab tech. I'm from Worcester, live here now." She had one of those brutal "Boston" accents, was a heavy-set woman with a chunky nondescript face, but a pair of soft and luminous, almost beseeching, brown eyes. Mary could see that she was stricken by shyness, and liked her immediately, irrationally; Sandy seemed more genuine than the other women.

The next woman to speak was Deb. She was plump and soft-looking, but with a strident manner. "Why aren't there any Third World women here?" was the first thing she said. "I'm Jewish, and I feel outnumbered. Is there anyone else Jewish here? Are you going to be able to relate to my experience of oppression?"

Alice motioned to say she was Jewish, but the facilitator broke in gently, "Maybe you could tell us a bit about yourself, Deb."

Deb hesitated. "I think I've said everything that's important, " she said abruptly.

Mary was counting in her head again. Three Jews, Jessica, Deb, and Alice; no waitresses. Was any of this important? Were lines being drawn somehow and different groups forming? Was she on the outside? And now, hideously, it was Mary's turn. "I'm Mary," she said, thinking how stupid her name sounded when said aloud. What should I say? she wondered frantically, then blurted out: "I just got divorced, and moved to Cambridge. I'm not sure what I'm doing with my life. I'm a waitress. My sister signed me up for this group!" Everyone laughed, but in a friendly way. "Oh, and I'm from the Island."

"Whoo . . ." Tish shook her hand, as if to imply that Mary must be one of the summer people, rich snobs.

"No, not like that, I mean we grew up there. Islanders. My parents ran the big supermarket. Well, maybe I'm not exactly an Islander because I wasn't born there, I was born in Natick when my folks lived out there for a few years, and Islanders don't really consider you to be an Islander unless your grandmother was born there . . ." She was running on, saying too much, and she'd humiliated herself. "Well, I'm here," she ended abruptly.

"Thank you," said Jessica, making her feel better. This left only the woman on Mary's left, who did not speak immediately. Mary took a peek at her, a tall, voluptuous woman, with high Slavic cheek bones and green eyes, light brown hair. She covered most of it with a large red kerchief, tied in back in an elaborate knot. She was the only woman in the room wearing a skirt, an old black one with a purple sweater drawn tightly across her large breasts. Mary couldn't tell if she was plain or beautiful. When she turned towards the group and began to speak, Mary decided she was beautiful.

"My name is Rania. I'm unemployed, and I'm looking for work. Do tell me if you know of a job! I was born in Cambridge, but my mother is Russian, my father from an old Cambridge family. They met in Paris after the war, are now divorced. I have three younger sisters. I live alone, which is important to me. And I'm not in a couple, which is also part of my identity. I notice people don't say if they were living with a lover."

"I'm not sure what you mean," said Tish. "I'm living in a communal house and I'm lovers with one of my roommates, but the situation isn't so clear cut."

"It's more an issue of solitude," said Rania, "I mean, not having many positive images of women living alone. Strong women are called spinsters, old maids, witches. I love living alone, in fact, I was going to invite this group to meet at my house next time; it might be more intimate."

"Maybe we could bring food," said Jessica, "I will, the first time, if someone will the next."

As everyone got up to leave, Mary felt strange, as if she'd briefly visited a foreign country. That night all the stupid things she had said went round and round in her head, a humiliating rerun of the meeting. Then she dreamed she and Rania were sledding downhill, in deep snow out of her Island childhood.

Chapter V

The Island has six towns, each separately incorporated, and of these the Harbor is the largest and the most developed. Here the Steamship Authority rules the port of entry, fixing fares and the number of visitors and cars — despotic, rude, and tardy, a venerable institution. Here the ferry disembarks and arrives, spewing out cars, trucks, and passengers at the slip, where the harbor makes a gentle cove, secure in all but the harshest weather for sailboats gently rocking at their moorings, for gulls sitting like sentries on the piers, and for children wading in the lapping waves. The Harbor, point of departure and reunion, lonesome as any port, with its implication of farewells and last embraces, the ferry sliding away from its locks, good-bye, good-bye.

As the winterized town of the Island, the Harbor houses everything that connects it in tribute to the great Commonwealth: the

Registry of Motor Vehicles, the two competing banks, the battered women's shelter, the Sears Roebuck. One summer, when the Island considered seceding from the Commonwealth, the Harbor was hung with flags of Independence: a white gull flying across an orange ball of sun, stitched to a sky or sea of blue.

Without anything particular to recommend it, the Harbor is still the place where everyone goes for everything: to buy nails or contraceptives, a new suit for an emergency wedding or funeral, a new pair of sunglasses for an emergency of unexpected good weather. It has the movie theater, the high school basketball game. In short, it is downtown, both loved and avoided. To hear Islanders talk, particularly summer folks of the more reclusive variety — temperamental poets or painters — the Harbor is 42nd Street, a den of iniquity, the fleshpots of Babylon, and a cacophony of traffic and noise. It is the only place on the Island that ever boasts of a traffic jam.

A LL THE HAIRS on Mary's arm stood up in goosebumps of attention. She was dancing wildly, pressed in a sway of bodies that vibrated to a woman's chilling voice, singing an old song with a new mystery.

Owl House was giving one of its famous parties. This one was for women only and was to celebrate the winter solstice. The living and dining rooms were lit by hundreds of votive candles that were set out in glasses, saucers, tea cups, candlesticks, candelabra, and bowls. Large platters held cut vegetables of all kinds — carrots, zucchini, and celery — and were strategically placed near equally large containers of unidentified dip that upon tasting proved to be hummus, cucumber, onion and sour cream, or baba ganosh. One roommate had made her famous zucchini bread, another had provided her famous hash brownies. Cheap wine, expensive grass, a little champagne, and a lot of poisonous-looking fruit punch flowed from hand to hand.

Both of the large Victorian-style rooms as well as the kitchen were packed with women chatting, flirting, and dancing madly. The heaviest crush was near the stereo speakers. Some friend of a friend had made this fantastic dancing tape. It could run for hours and exhaust them all in the process. Mary wasn't sure who she was dancing with, but she was dancing, feeling her center of gravity drop, her hips take on a rhythm of their own, her hair fly out electric, her eyes half closed, her hands invoke the fluttering wings of birds. Dancing, she was dazzled. Her heart called to some wild goddess to come down and dance inside her.

Therese and Lu were slow dancing to a fast song, cheek to cheek, their lips brushing occasionally. Lu was small, but she made Therese feel safe; when Therese put her arms around her, she felt as if it was she who was the little one, the cozy baby.

"This next song is for Lu. Hey, Lu!" yelled out the friend of the friend who had made the tape. She'd put on everyone's requests and favorites, which made for an odd mix at times, Bette Midler with Lou Reed, Aretha Franklin with Holly Near, two obscure versions of "Louie, Louie," even a hideously misogynist Rolling Stones song, along with the more predictable Bonnie Raitt and Chris Williamson. Lu's song was one of the few reggae songs, Bob Marley singing "I shot the sheriff" in a version that must have been a dozen years old. Therese could never quite figure out why this was Lu's favorite song. Was Lu planning to shoot a cop? This seemed out of character. Was there even a sheriff to be shot in the Cambridge-Somerville area? And was this somehow meant to be politically correct?

Actually, Therese's favorite song was Stevie Wonder's "You are the sunshine of my life," but torture would not reveal this fact from her. And there was Lu, blithely whirling her around, doing some strange cha-cha step only known to junior high girls in California, and yelling along with the song. Therese liked that, and Lu kissed her in sheer exuberance.

Mary was dancing, stoned on punch and the two hits of a joint passed her. Two women were giving each other shotgun hits of grass, blowing the smoke directly into each other's mouths; Mary hadn't seen anything like that in years. Mary wasn't sure who she was dancing with, but she knew who it was she was trying to dance with. She squeezed through the crowd until she spotted Rania, who was wearing of all things a black sheath dress with rhinestones and a pair of red stockings. The dress was from the Thirties, and her hair was tied up in a matching black silk scarf. She looked like a Gypsy dressed for a cocktail party. They began to dance, not so much with each other as at each other, shaking their hips and flirting their finger tips. By now, Patti Smith was singing "Gloria," that girl's name drawn out to the ecstasy of a hallelujah chorus, and the crowd was singing and shouting too. Rania took Mary's hand.

Therese dipped a mushroom in sour cream and put it in Lu's mouth. Lu was trying unsuccessfully to coax the house cats, who were hidden in panic beneath the big couches. Red wine was spilled on the kitchen table. Women were starting to leave with women they hadn't arrived with. The neighbors called the cops, who insisted the music be turned down. It was 2 AM, and still the party showed no signs of abating.

"You can sleep at my house," Rania said to Mary. "This party is going to go on until tomorrow and you'll never be able to get to sleep here."

Mary was relieved. The same thought had occurred to her and she'd been about to ask Therese and Lu if she could crash with them, but their look of romantic insularity held her back. She didn't want to intrude, and being with lovers made her too lonely. Now here was an adventure: Rania. Was Rania making a pass at her? Or was it just a kindly Good Samaritan offer? Maybe Rania was lonely, too, but how much difference was there between a pass and loneliness? Mary didn't care at that moment. "I'd love to," she said.

They didn't talk in Rania's decrepit blue VW, which reminded Mary of the one she'd left behind on the Island, drained, and up on blocks in the back yard, hibernating for the winter. She wondered idly at the love between women of her generation and VW bugs. This one didn't have much heat, and once out on the snowy streets Mary felt her high wear off, replaced by a slug of fatigue. Rania did not seem inclined to make conversation. She smoked and drove with the concentration of someone who suspects sheet ice and the arrival of the police. And yet, like all Boston drivers, she drove insanely, methodically running each yellow or barely red light, taking a calm left turn out of the right hand lane. At least she wasn't going sixty down the narrow Somerville streets.

Somerville, which the sign proudly proclaimed had once been named "The All America City," looked bleak in the winter dark, a town of small squares and cramped houses,

Cambridge's dowdy relation to all but her residents, who felt a kind of peace in her honest blunt neighborhoods and old trees. Rania's building was dark and ugly, a brick square in an obscure corner of the city. Inside the apartment it was freezing, and Rania made Mary nervous by turning on the oven for heat; she was sure the fumes would suffocate them both. The oven did heat the entire place, which was only one largish room, with an alcove for a kitchen. Mercifully it was free of cats and political posters. There was only a bright rag rug on the linoleum floor, a white wicker rocking chair, and on the wall behind it, a large realistic painting of a white rocking chair. The bed dominated one corner, with a red spread and a dozen small pillows and shawls scattered over it.

Somehow Rania's house spoke of poverty to Mary, not that it was in any a worse neighborhood than her own, or more peculiarly furnished than Therese's, or smaller than her Island shack. Maybe it was the linoleum floor that she knew would be cold if she got up in the middle of the night to pee. Then she realized that what she was reacting to was that Rania lived alone. No one made any noise unless she made it, no one came in or out unless she did, no one ate the food in the refrigerator but she. Mary felt terrified. A kind of vertigo swept over her, the vertigo that she'd fled the Island to avoid, a sensation of being totally alone in cold space. Then she realized that Rania was asking her something: would she like to borrow a nightgown? did she mind sleeping in the bed? It was warmer with two people anyway. Mary said yes, yes, vaguely, and escaped to the bathroom.

Once in bed, it was warmer, and in the dark Mary began to relax. She could feel her heart beating, and she wondered if Rania was going to kiss her. She could not actually bring herself to kiss Rania first. And then Rania did kiss her, leaning over slowly and surely and taking her chin in her hand. The kiss was warm and calm. The rest of the love-making, though, had a tentative quality that was more shy than erotic. Mary liked Rania's breasts, but much of Rania puzzled her. She couldn't tell . . . how hard, how soft, to ask a question, to remain silent; she remained silent. She thought maybe Rania came, but Mary didn't, and Rania did not ask.

The next morning, the linoleum floor was as cold as Mary had expected, and she was slightly hung over. The whole room looked frighteningly clear and bright in the morning sun. It felt late but it was only 7 AM. Still, they got up anyway. Because there was nothing in the refrigerator except two beers, some butter, and a largish piece of brie cheese — this last striking Mary as an odd extravagance — Mary simply went home to her own house for breakfast, taking two buses and waiting out on the ice. Mary and Rania had kissed gently goodbye in a way that informed Mary of nothing. Was this a one night stand? Would she sleep with Rania again? Did she want to?

Mary was inwardly shocked that she had made love with a woman, however low-keyed that love had been. She felt suddenly sharp in her own outline, radically cut off from her usual surroundings, more distinct, separate. She stood in the cold wishing that she had gloves and waiting for the next bus to come.

Sensibly, Mary did not mention the Rania incident — as she began to refer to it — to Therese. Therese would have jumped to conclusions, to rhetoric, to generally dominating the situation with her theories and her glee. However, just as she could not tell Therese, she could also not tell Elizabeth or Cathy, who would look at her as if she were going to pounce on them and as if she were a traitor to their family cause of heterosexuality, now that she was a lez-bee-anne. Mary wasn't sure who she was, she suspected that had less to do with sex than her sisters would believe.

And besides, the next time she was over at Therese and Lu's they were having a horrible fight, proof that women with women were no more immune to craziness than women with men.

"You can't," shrieked Therese at Lu.

"Can't what?" Mary was embarrassed to have walked in on a scene, but her curiosity made the best of it.

"She says I can't apply to medical school in California," said Lu, calm but white-faced.

"Why not?"

Therese answered: "I hate California. I hate and despise it. I won't go. I absolutely refuse to leave Boston."

"You'd love northern California," said Lu.

"No. I'd hate it. All the lesbians wear purple and no one has any politics."

"But hot tubs! Eucalyptus trees! Sushi bars."

"I hate sushi."

"You love sushi."

"I'm becoming a vegetarian. Leave me alone."

"You're becoming a pain in the ass."

"Then go without me."

"Okay, I will. I have a career to think of. You should learn to make some compromises. You're selfish. Your whole goddamned family is selfish, a bunch of humorless self-engrossed . . ."

At this point Mary departed hastily. As soon as she left Therese was reduced to yelling "Fuck you!" at Lu, who regarded her with disgust.

"Fuck you, too," said Lu, in a prim voice, and left the room.

Therese then set to work with a hammer and smashed an entire set of dishes, methodically and with some pleasure. They were green plastic dishes no one ever used, having been left by the previous tenants, who purchased them with plaid stamps. Still, Therese felt better for a moment, but then realized that she would need to break more than the dishes to feel completely better. She felt her rage inside her like a fierce iron pole poking into her stomach, freezing her spine.

Lu sat in the bedroom, feeling an odd mixture of relief and despair. Half consciously, she was cutting up a piece of paper with the nail scissors. She felt relief because she had decided to go to California without Therese, preferably immediately, and she felt hysterical because she was deeply in love with someone who was behaving badly and even throwing a temper tantrum in the next room. How could she, Lu, who was both rational and kind-hearted, love Therese, who at the moment was neither? But then a knock came on the bedroom door, and Therese was saying "Lu?" rather plaintively. They embraced and apologized, although each continued to nurse her wrongs for a while. Therese, reverting to childhood, simply put the whole thing out of her mind. Lu, however, without telling Therese directly, applied to fifteen medical schools — seven in California, two in New York, and the rest in or near Boston.

The next time Mary's women's group met she had a small anxiety attack beforehand, and took special care of her appearance. Perhaps it was the prospect of seeing Rania again, particularly in Rania's apartment, that provoked her primping. That is, she wore her usual outfit but had washed it carefully, including her hair. She peered out at herself in the foggy bathroom mirror and saw a pretty woman squinting at herself. Mary had always been considered the "artistic" one, the "sensitive" sister. This translated as the hippie, the incompetent, the moody one. It was Therese who in childhood had been the "pretty" one, Therese who now dressed and stood like a street urchin, Therese who could still look tall and svelte wrapped in a bath towel but whose sullen expression on the subject of feminine charm also served to obscure her own charm. Therese who had been "pretty" and was now "angry": as in, "Oh, I just can't talk to Therese any more, and she flies off the handle at the slightest thing. And we can't all be expected to live her lifestyle!" Mary privately thought of Therese as "fierce"; and yet wasn't Elizabeth supposed to be the fierce one — the sexy, incorrigible one, the cigarette-smoking one, the one who was kicked out of a high school dance because her mini skirt was too short, the dark-haired one. Men seemed to find her irresistible, her black hair shining like a beacon among her sisters' mass of blonde. But how did this image jibe with reality: Elizabeth the intellectual, the Harvard teaching fellow, the brilliant one, the one who believed that reliving the past in therapy could actually change someone, the one who believed the same thing about art and literature and love? And yet Mary knew that Elizabeth regarded herself as the only sensible one of the lot, the one with common sense, the only one who paid her parking tickets, who used her diaphragm conscientiously, who had good taste in clothes and allegedly good taste in men. But Howard? A man who threw a stereo amplifier through a closed window could hardly be considered a good catch. Well, now there was Jed, the perfect, the adorable, although Mary found him both too short for her taste and too self-engrossed, a bit pedantic, even. Therese persisted in seeing Elizabeth as a battered woman while Elizabeth now saw herself as saved by love, hardly the intellectual position. And where did this leave little Cathy in the family constellation? "Little" Cathy with her condo and new car and sailing club and a desk at the bank with her name on it and her investments and her three-piece suits and her dresser drawers full of lacy underwear. Certainly she was the only one in the family who really acted like an adult woman, who would have pleased either of her long-dead grandmothers. She would go far, but not too far, little Cathy, the nice one, Daddy's sweetheart, with her bitchy tongue, her pushy manner with headwaiters. Cathy, the invisible one, the caboose at the end of the Little Women train, now all grown-up.

Mary stopped squinting at herself and brooding about her family in time to motivate herself toward the women's group. She wanted to be a bit late, and avoid meeting Rania alone in her cold apartment. But when she arrived, the apartment was warm and smelled cosily of coffee, and only Jessica and Tish were already there. Jessica was laying out the cheese and crackers she had brought, along with a loaf of banana bread. Tish and Rania were sitting together on the sofa, laughing together intimately, looking deep into each other's eyes. And they did present a picture, Mary had to admit, both so fair with their pixie haircuts, Rania voluptuous and Tish with her heart-shaped face.

Luckily, however, the rest of the group arrived almost immediately, and the mood between the two on the couch was broken. Rania looked up and smiled at Mary a bit mistily.

"Shall we start?" asked Jessica, passing the banana bread. "Is everyone here?"

"Deb isn't here," said Sandy, "but I'm not sure if she will be, she didn't seem too comfortable. Do you think we could have made her more comfortable?"

"It's hard to speculate on that," said Jessica, "maybe we could agree that in the future no one will leave without telling the group first."

Mary felt trapped. There was nothing in her life, now that she couldn't leave without warning, but she nodded along with everyone else.

"I have some topics," said Jessica. "Why don't we pick some for the next few weeks? How about mothers, sexuality, racism, class, men, work . . . anything else?"

"Living alone," said Rania.

"Money," said Tish.

"Isn't that class?" asked Rania.

The group finally settled on sexuality, mothers, and racism for the next three meetings. Mary couldn't decide if the topics got easier or harder. But the group seemed eager to start with sex. Alice waved her hand and said, "I have a problem with this, so can I begin?"

"Sure."

"Well," she said in her soft voice, "when I first got trained to work on the railroad, I'd considered myself a lesbian for at least ten years. I mean, in high school I went out with men, but not after that. And I was really involved in the women's community here. When I and the women got trained we heard that the railroad workers' wives were upset that there would be women on the crew. They thought we might steal their husbands away. We thought this was pretty funny because we were both dykes! Now I've been on the railroad over a year, and I feel out of touch with the women's community. I'm tired at night and I don't go out to the bars or dancing or something as much as I used to. Plus, there's this guy I work with who is really nice. I mean, we both work with the union, he's just about my age and we like a lot of the same things. We went to a couple of basketball games together and I was pretty attracted to him and before I really considered it I was sleeping with him!"

"Do you like it?" asked Tish, perky but rude.

"Well, yes, and I like him a lot, I mean, he's a very sweet guy."

"Does he know about you?"

"Yes, but it doesn't seem important. It's just important to me. I mean, what am I? Who am I?"

"Well, it seems . . ."

"Excuse me," interjected Jessica. "If Alice is done, why don't we go around and give everyone a chance to speak before we throw the conversation open. Is that okay, Alice?"

"Sure. I feel better just saying it."

"Next?"

"I'll go," said Sandy. "Alice, your story touched me, even though I'm a lesbian and always have been and always will be. I knew from the time I was very young that I was different from other people, but it took me a while to figure out how. For me, being a lesbian is just who I am, more than just sexuality. Right now I'm alone. Sometimes I think I'd like a lover, but sometimes I think I'm not over the last one." Sandy stopped abruptly, afraid she'd said too much too soon. "That's all, thank you."

Touched, Mary responded: "I'm the same way, too. Sexuality? I'm not even sure what mine is, aside from specific people. I was married for a long time . . ."

"How long?" interrupted Tish.

"Too long! I'd gone out with him since high school and married him in college. We just separated. When I was married there wasn't really sexuality, I mean, there was sex, of course, good and bad sex, and wondering if he was messing around or if I should, but now that I'm alone, there's sort of an issue, capital S sex, as if people keep expecting me to behave one way or the other, be on the make, or . . . or . . . "

"But you would rather listen to what's inside you, and you're not exactly sure what that is," said Jessica.

"Yes, that's it." What a relief to be understood. Then Mary was suddenly and horribly conscious of Rania sitting across the circle from her. What would she make of all this? Mary had spoken spontaneously, without caution. For a moment she had forgotten that she had made love with a woman sitting in that very room.

Tish said, "For me, it's a matter of a particular person, although I'm pretty sure I want that other person to be a woman. But my lover, the one I live in the group house with, and I are in a kind of crisis. We can't decide whether or not to be monogamous, whether we should start seeing other people." Mary watched Tish look up and smile directly at Rania. "Sometimes I think we should just commit ourselves to each other, maybe get an apartment alone together. You know, sex is really where we're compatible, very cuddly and all, but she and I don't agree that much about politics. I mean I'm politically active and my lover resents the time away from her, even something like tonight." Tish fell silent, more genuine than she had been all evening.

Jessica waited a moment until she was sure Tish was done, and then said, "For me, sexuality is all tied up with my family, my emotions. When my mother died I didn't want to make love at all for months . . ."

"Me too! I mean, when my father died. Joe just couldn't understand. He kept saying a good fuck would cure me. But I felt, I don't know, hollow somehow, transparent, as if my body wasn't quite there. Oh, I'm sorry, I'm interrupting."

But Jessica nodded at Mary, "No, thank you. I felt the same way. I like men, I like my boyfriend, but I like living alone, too. But I've never been able to separate sex from my mood. Sometimes I feel as if everyone is having really great orgasms all the time except me . . ."

Everyone began to laugh, Alice so hard that she had to put her face down in her hands. "Okay, okay," Jessica was laughing, too. "But you know what I mean. Well, I'm done. I feel better, too."

This left only Rania. Everyone was looking at her expectantly. She was looking at her hands. Then she said, "I want to pass. I don't feel comfortable talking here."

"Are you sure?" said Jessica. "Can we make you feel safer?"

"No," said Rania, "really, I'd just rather not."

Tish patted her shoulder gently. Mary felt her stomach clench. Was she jealous? Something didn't seem fair, but she wasn't sure what. She was glad when the conversation went back to Alice's problem and how she could keep relating to the women's community even if she was seeing the cute guy from the railroad. Mary didn't quite understand why it was all a problem, but then, she reasoned, things like this didn't usually happen on the Island.

The whole next week Mary did not hear from Rania, not that it was clear that she should have. The idea of another meeting, however, without clearing the air between them, was upsetting. Besides, that Tuesday Mary just didn't want to go to her group. They were supposed to talk about their mothers, and she didn't think she could stand mothers at the moment, cruel mothers, vicarious mothers, drunken mothers, suffocating mothers, dead mothers, internalized mothers, Jewish mothers, Catholic mothers, lesbian mothers, witch mothers, tooth mothers, mothers that lurked in the night and then pounced on you with their hair streaming and eyes burning, or just ordinary daylight mothers, bringing you a glass of ginger ale with a bendable straw because you were home sick and got to watch television.

It was all too confusing. She called Elizabeth but Jed said that Elizabeth was at her group, a new therapy one, so she then called Rania, her fingers feeling numb as she dialed the number.

"Rania?"

"Yes."

"This is Mary."

"Oh."

"Are you going to the group tonight?"

"No, I don't think so."

"Why don't we go out for a beer and play hooky together and we'll talk about our mothers anyway?"

"I haven't eaten. If you want, I'll pick you up and we can get some dinner."

They went to one of the intimate soup places that Rania frequented, just enough off the beaten Harvard track to be cozy and deep enough into Somerville to be run by some collective or other of ferocious-looking women and sweet bearded men who appeared in touch with their feelings at all costs, even when they were dominating a meeting. Their order was taken by a waiter who then went off to have a crisis with a bisexual poet, and forty-five minutes later they got a huge Greek salad they hadn't ordered, along with their cups of black bean soup. By now they were ravenous, and the new waitress said it was on the house.

Rania stopped chain smoking and nibbled a lettuce leaf. She looked voluptuous, with the unhealthy color of a still young woman whose calories come more from liquor than from solid food.

"Tell me about your mother," said Mary, buttering a piece of bread all over the front of her sweater. Being with Rania was making her nervous. "What is she like?"

"My mother," said Rania, "is the barely legitimate daughter of two White Russian refugees who met in Paris. That is, my grandfather married my grandmother when she was in her ninth month, although they never lived together, as he lived with his mistress. My grandmother actually was the illegitimate daughter of a beautiful serf and a Russian nobleman."

Mary couldn't tell if Rania was lying, but she didn't care; she was fascinated. Her mother could hardly compare to Rania's, but Rania asked her anyway.

"Oh, my mother . . ." said Mary.

"Does she look like you? Or rather, do you look like her?"

"Sort of, only she's shorter, but she still dyes her hair to a kind of dirty blonde like mine. I think her features are more like Cathy's — that's my youngest sister — I mean they both have broad smiles and kind of wide cheekbones."

"Does she work? My mother has never worked a day in her life, unless you count living off men as work, which in a way it is. First she lived with my father, and as he's a depressive and a WASP, that must have been hard work! And now she lives off a series of lovers."

"You mean men pay her?" Mary sounded a little shocked, despite her intention of acting worldly wise. This was beyond her experience.

"Not exactly. Not that crass. She's more in the mistress category, you know . . . some married man sets her up in an apartment and visits every Tuesday and Thursday. Another buys her clothes, or sends her to the Bahamas for vacation. She gets by. Besides, she has the alimony."

"Work! Matty, my mother, has always worked. God, how she impressed that one on us, her tales of babysitting practically as soon as she could toddle. Then she was a waitress all through high school; worked summers as a maid, cleaning houses, other people's dirty messes; then she went to work at Filene's, which was a fancy job in those days for someone like her, and after she married my father, why, she never stopped working, first the store out in Natick, and then the bigger store on the Island, plus the four babies, one after another in as many years, and all the housekeeping, seeing as my father never so much as washed a dish."

"Is she bitter?" Rania wanted to know.

"Bitter? No; why, not at all. Proud of herself, of course, and maybe disappointed in us. None of her children have that kind of drive. Cathy's doing well, and Elizabeth will go far, but Matty doesn't really understand that kind of work. And we all get the flu and headaches and depressed when we're overtired, and she's never been sick, not as I can remember. Besides, not one of us has a kid, let alone four. Can you imagine, she was a mother of four at my age! We're soft compared to her."

"She sounds like a tough lady," said Rania, and then added pensively, "You know, I'm terrified that I'll turn into my mother, all soft and dependent, unable to fend for myself. That's why I live alone; but I'm not doing too well in the employment department."

"Any luck finding work?"

"Just temporary stuff. Typing. I start to feel like I'm suffocating, trapped in an office like that."

"Are you going to stay in the group, go back next week? I liked the discussion on sex. I just couldn't handle talking about mothers this time."

"No, I don't think so. Are you?"

"Yeah, guess I am. My sister Therese thinks it's good for me. I'm not sure if that's the case, but I like it, hearing what each person says. It's sort of like reading a novel. I want to see how each story comes out."

"I'm thinking of getting a teaching credential," said Rania, changing the subject abruptly.

"Really? Maybe that will work out for you."

"Maybe, but you know what a wreck the Boston schools are. I am on the substitute list, though." Rania spoke abstractedly, and picked up Mary's hand. Mary tingled: she hadn't expected Rania to touch her. Then Rania put Mary's hand in her mouth, like a cat picking up a kitten, and began to nibble on her fingertips.

They paid the check hastily, and Mary insisted on her house, even though she knew it needed cleaning. She just couldn't face the linoleum in Rania's cold apartment, or the two bus rides back in the snow.

They lay down together on Mary's bed under the quilt fully clothed, and began kissing passionately and stroking each other's hair. Suddenly Rania sat bolt upright and looked at the clock. It was only 8:30 P.M.

"My medicine!" she exclaimed, and went into a long unconvincing riff about some antibiotics she was taking for a urinary tract infection. Mary didn't believe her, but it was obvious Rania wanted to leave. Mary saw her to the door, and then got back under the quilt with all her clothes still on.

It was too early to go to sleep but she turned out the lights anyway. She knew she had seen the last of Rania.

Chapter VI

Around the lagoon and to the east of the Harbor lies the the town of The Bluffs, scene of the camp meetings in the previous century, and still containing a wild array of gingerbread Victorian houses, painted ladies in brilliant colors, trimmed in wooden lace, carved with cookie cutter stars and moons, with a rocking chair on every porch. The bandstand sits serenely on the green, delicate as an ornamental bird cage, waiting to fill the evening air with the imported strains of jazz or the national anthem under a sky of fireworks. One can walk along the seawall there, past jetties and sea debris, in the slight melancholy of the nostalgic scene. The Bluffs, with its rooming houses and crooked streets, is the only place on the Island to come close to one of those decrepit Atlantic seaside towns, those rainy-day places with boardwalks and arcades. The Bluffs is home for the few Island drifters, for the more temporary and less well-heeled tourists, for the rows of pinball and video games, and for the carousel, turning, eternal, complete with a free ride for anyone who can grab the golden ring.

THERESE FELT THAT IT WAS IMPORTANT to have official policies in this life; having a position forced other people to take one seriously. Therese's current official position on going to Berkeley with Lu was that she refused to go somewhere where all the women had changed their names to Moonwoman or Mountain; she also claimed to hate burritos. Therese insisted that if she left Harvard Square she would shrivel up, become invisible, perhaps even die. She insisted that she loved scrod, whatever that was, and did not feel alive if she wasn't within walking distance of the Atlantic, and smoke-filled rooms where proper Boston dykes fought over socialist-feminism. Therese claimed that she had to be able to go clam digging to feel safe, at home in the universe, and ditto for throwing a brick or two through the plate glass windows of the Square.

But like many official policies, Therese's did not present the whole truth. And when Therese was being honest with herself she remembered that she adored to travel, was the only one of the sisters who had ever been anywhere. Indeed, she loved to travel as much as she loved to stay home in Boston, printing manifestos and eating chocolate jimmies on her ice cream cones.

When Therese's father — and she, like all of her sisters, thought of him as her property alone — had died, they had each received a substantial sum, composed of his life insurance, some inheritance, and some of their mother's share which she had generously passed on to them at the time. "I don't want you sitting around waiting for me to die," said Matty in a brittle tone she reserved for affectionate acts. Each sister had reacted characteristically to the bequest. Cathy had put down a deposit on her condo and begun to play the market, a bit conservatively but rather successfully at that. Elizabeth had lived off it bit by bit, financing graduate school before she got her fellowship, paying her therapist (but still low on the sliding scale), squandering some now and then on clothes, and frittering away ghastly sums at chic Harvard

Square cafes. Elizabeth had never meant it to last, which was fine; she had an academic future and a man from the middle class. Therese had also played the grasshopper rather than the ant. Mary, however, had played some typically ineffectual combination of the two by choosing the shack and land out of her father's estate rather than cash, becoming land rich and virtually penniless in one swoop.

Therese had spent her money in wandering about the wide world. She spent six months in Latin America, mostly in Peru, among mountains and political coups. She spent a summer in Israel with her gorgeous yet dogmatic Zionist girlfriend. That had been her most serious relationship before Lu, a woman who had actually been one of her freshman roommates at Radcliffe. Therese had also taken Lu to visit Matty in the Caribbean last winter, and she'd gone to Cuba semi-legally on a tour sponsored by a Bulgarian travel agency. Now, unfortunately but hardly surprisingly, the cash was dwindling. There was just enough for two people to take a modest little trip, say two weeks at Christmas to the Grand Canyon, or to take the train to Seattle, or maybe a quick jaunt to Mexico, although that might have been stretching it. But what should she do? Lu was going home for the holidays to Berkeley, ostensibly to see her family, but Therese suspected that she also had a medical school interview. They had agreed to curtail all arguments until the facts were in — and this seemed reasonable because there were no more dishes left to break. Therese was left with a sense of unease, an anxiety that underlay her waking mind, waiting to ambush her.

No, she didn't want to go with Lu to California. Maybe Mary would like to go somewhere. They were getting along all right. And even though Mary seemed better, no doubt she could still use some cheering up. Elizabeth and Cathy were hopelessly entwined with their men. She doubted if Elizabeth even took a pee without having Jed in the bathroom for company. And Cathy and whatshisname were probably going off to some cute resort in the Berkshires, ye olde inn with a roaring yule log in the fireplace. Therese was being unchari-table, and knew it, but was enjoying herself too much to stop.

Still, Mary was okay. The question now was one of desti-nation. The Southwest sounded good, it conjured up mescaline-colored deserts, but the Grand Canyon was a bit too . . . not exactly commercial, maybe just too much of a picture postcard. Santa Fe? Supposed to be nice. Chaco Canyon? Wasn't that where they had some kind of solstice calendar and miles of roads and probably a matriarchal civilization? Therese wanted to see an Anasazi city carved in rock or rising from a plain. But she'd heard that Chaco was impassible this time of year. Well, she would get some guide books.

Therese daydreamed all afternoon at the press, traveling far even as she was sitting at the light table. There'd been a big rush job at the Women's Press this morning, one that was already a day late, but they'd finally finished the damn thing. And there was supposed to be some kind of knockdown drag out fight at the meeting tonight, something about censorship. The afternoon was sunny and quiet. Therese drank the bitter dregs of her styrofoam cup of coffee and nibbled on the remains of a jelly doughnut. Lu would kill her if she could see her eating like that, but Therese always enjoyed a doughnut. Her father Al used to say, "If these cost as much as caviar, everyone would enjoy them properly." He had liked the Boston cream kind. Therese knew she shouldn't be eating and pasting up at the same time, but she was neat and quick. She liked her work, precise and laborious. It took her out of herself the way nothing else did, except maybe riding her bicycle.

On the supper break before the meeting, Therese did bicycle to the Square, cautious in the slush and snow. The drivers were insane. Boston must be the only place in the country where cars pass on both the right and left, where stop signs are an invitation to speed up, and where the hapless pedestrian is seen as a moving target. The traffic lights shone garishly on the snow; the brightly lit shops seemed to accentuate the cold and dark outside. The Christmas decorations made Therese feel forlorn. A VW Bug cut her off. "Up yours!" yelled Therese, winding her way in and out of traffic. Then she saw something that made her want to get off her bicycle and cry. On one of the trestles that the MBTA was using to segregate its construction area, someone had spraypainted, in large orange letters, NIGGERS SUCK. Therese felt sick. She hated Boston, racist, violent, worse than the South before civil rights, a place where no one ever felt safe a block out of their own neighborhood. And this right in Harvard Square, a place that was supposed to be immune, her own neighborhood.

She couldn't do anything about it at the moment, though, without spray paint and in traffic, so she turned into the bookstore, chaining her bicycle to a lamppost outside. The store smelled of drying rubber boots and steaming wool, but there was nothing more comforting to Therese than shelves and shelves of books, travel books in particular. She ended up buying maps of the entire Four Corners area, and after her meeting, which inspired homicide in her and her fellow press women, went home to bed to peruse the *Mobil Travel Guide*.

"The *Mobil Travel Guide?*" said Lu, in her most facetiously holistic tone. Lu was on her side of the bed, barricaded in with pillows and a pile of books that included a collection of T'ang Dynasty poets and a tome on "spiritual midwifery." Actually, Lu was secretly reading her favorite back section of the *Boston Globe*, "Confidential Chat," which was a soothing compendium of readers' recipes and advice about bedwetting toddlers. "I have just moved to a new city in the Midwest because of my husband's business and I miss my old friends. Maybe the Chat could give me some advice about how to meet . . . " Lu read aloud to an indifferent Therese.

"The *Mobil Guide* is good," insisted Therese. "It gives you all kinds of great information. Like, it tells you right here that there's a motel on the rim of Canyon de Chelly, run by Navajos, with a good cafeteria, open Christmas Day."

"Don't they rate things with little forks?"

"Yeah, well . . . what you're reading doesn't look that intellectual, either."

"Ah, le Chat Confidential," said Lu to one of the cats, as it jumped on the bed and snuggled into her afghan. "Come here."

Therese took this as an invitation. "You come here," she said to Lu, kissing her passionately and attempting to drag her, cat, and afghan onto her side of the bed. They might not trust each other completely, thought Therese, but at least their bodies still worked together.

A few days later Therese stopped in to visit Mary unexpectedly. Mary was making herself up to go to work. Therese watched disapprovingly as she squinted into the wavy mirror above the dresser, applying brown eyeliner and a bit of purple shadow. Therese determined to take her away from all this.

"Canyon de what?" asked Mary.

"Canyon de Chelly, it's very beautiful. We fly to Albuquerque, rent a car, it's easy. Drive up to Canyon de Chelly, maybe go to a few pueblos on the way. Come back through Santa Fe. Gorgeous. Not too crowded. Not too hot this time of year. Perfect. We'll have a great time. Leave Christmas Eve, avoid all that holiday bullshit. It'll be great."

"Therese, I'm broke. Totally broke. It's fine for you to talk but I need to try and save and I have less than a . . . "

"I'm paying."

"You're what?"

"I'm paying. My treat. I'll take you, I'm taking you to Canyon de Chelly for New Year's, for Christ's sake. So come on!"

"Therese . . ."

"What?"

"I can't. This is crazy. You're too nice."

"This is uncharacteristic reticence," said Therese, snippiness making her polysyllabic.

"Oh, honey, I didn't mean to offend you. It's a wonderful idea, it's just, I mean I can't, in good conscious, the money is yours and you should use it . . ."

"Good, it's settled," Therese was beaming again. "We're going! It's all set. Just bring warm clothes and a pair of rubber boots, because the river at the bottom of the canyon is sometimes flooded."

"You're crazy," said Mary. But she embraced her, holding her longer than any of the sisters usually did.

The night before they planned to leave, Therese got up at four in the morning and bicycled to the Square. It was so cold she imagined the breath freezing in her lungs, but all that happened was that it hung like a cloud of smoke before her.

Armed with a can of purple spray paint, she confronted NIGGERS SUCK, and erased it in sticky swirls. But this wasn't quite enough. The finger on the trigger itched for more. What should she write? She'd always admired those bizarre poems painted on the walls near MIT: "Pull this change, ungloved hand, no boundary," and the like. Suddenly, it came to her. She wrote in purple foot-high letters:

RAINBOW IS ENOUGH. Therese was satisfied; she was becoming the secret guerilla fighter of Harvard Square, a protector of the peace, vigilante, poet.

On Christmas Eve day Mary and Therese took the T and a series of shuttle buses to Logan Airport. Mary almost could not believe that she was going somewhere, going anywhere, and that she was saved from Christmas. It was snowing slightly, but the flight went off as scheduled. When they landed in Albuquerque it was nightfall, and lights glittered in the desert below them.

In the Albuquerque airport everything looked different, somehow fresh, foreign. There were men wearing cowboy hats and enormous belt buckles made of inlaid turquoise. Indian motifs were painted on the walls. Everyone seemed to be smiling and moving slowly, and it was almost warm outside. Then Mary panicked. Outside! Once she left the airport, she would be out, out there, in the big desert, the enormous void of space that wasn't Boston, and even more wasn't the Island. Her knees buckled, and she was afraid she was going to vomit as she struggled toward the ladies' room.

Once in the stall she put her head down between her knees and after a few moments felt better. She pulled out her old lipstick and wondered what to write on the wall. She considered writing BOSTON BOSTON, but thought better of it, and wrote her name: MARY and then her married name, which she still went by. Then she wrote her Island address: WEST BEERSHEBA, MA 02535. It looked very official, her return address, and she felt considerably happier.

Where were they going to sleep that night? "Therese . . . " she implored, back in the baggage claim area. But Therese was briskly gathering up their suitcases, dialing a phone on a board that was plastered with pictures of hotels, talking, smiling, and reporting to Mary, "Come on! We can get a motel shuttle bus right outside to the Payless Motel."

"Payless?" Mary was beginning to feel amused.

"Stop it." Therese was laughing herself. "It's close, and cheap, and we don't have the car until tomorrow morning."

The last time Mary had been in a motel had been during the storm at Wood's Hole. The Payless was bland but pleasant, and beyond the low motel with its small turquoise swimming pool there was the desert, the sea of the desert, the great dome of night choked with stars, rivers and canyons, arroyos and flash floods, gigantic cactus reaching skyward with stars caught in needles and branches, adobe houses with piñon logs scenting the air, and then Mexico, with piñatas and luminarias lighting up the Christmas dark, children dressed like Mary and Joseph, and that was in the desert too, wilderness, forty days and forty nights, anyway it was beautiful in the desert at night, and it was still Christmas Eve.

"Merry Christmas," Mary said to Therese. But Therese was already asleep.

In the morning, Albuquerque looked like Somerville plunked down in the middle of nowhere. It was just a strip, with hamburger joints and plastic Christmas decorations strung across the street. But it wasn't Somerville, and they were eating huevos rancheros, which Mary couldn't even pronounce, for breakfast. The eggs were delicious, and there was also some kind of cactus jelly for the biscuits, but Mary wouldn't eat it, although Therese insisted it didn't taste as green as it looked.

They were strangers in this place, which is why Therese had come. She wanted to be foreign, exotic, lost again. She wanted an adventure, not skydiving or sexual infidelity, but an adventure of a new world. Therese suspected that if she were really a successful traveler she could make the world come new again even in Harvard Square. But she wasn't up to that yet. She still needed to start from a foreign place.

They set out in the rented car, Therese driving, even though Mary considered her to be an inferior driver. However, it was Therese's credit card. And Therese could follow the map, heading toward Acoma, under the enormous sky, cloud-massed, with the blue and tan mesas beneath it, and the red earth. Therese knew from reading her guide books that this desert had once been warm Cambrian seas, and she imagined this early, ancient scene with the rising mesas as thousands of islands. Now they were wind-carved rocks sailing across the desert.

"Acoma," Therese told Mary, "is a pueblo built high on a mesa, for defense. The Spanish did manage to take it, though, and they set up a priest on the rock. After many years, one night all the inhabitants took him and threw him off the cliff!"

Therese sighed with pleasure at this romantic and anti-imperialist piece of history. But Mary was simply staring out the window, drugged with the wonder of the landscape. She was thinking about one of the books she had brought to read, one with "Zen" in the title and an open circle of Japanese ink on the cover.

"Therese?"

"Hmm . . ."

"Have you ever read anything about Buddhism?"

"Nope. Religion is the opiate, and all that. Besides, isn't it very nihilistic or something?" Much as she tried to hide it, Therese's Harvard education still showed.

"Well, Buddhism, I mean this book I'm reading, says life is suffering, that's the basis of it all, life is just suffering. Do you think so? I mean, is life just suffering? It certainly is some of the time. Do you know?"

Therese said slowly, "Yeah, sure, life is suffering." Then paused and laughed: "But you should ask someone who isn't half Irish Catholic and a lesbian!" She laughed again.

"This book says that life is sickness, old age, and death."

"Gross," said Therese, and turned on the radio. When they came to Acoma the steep road led them upward through drifts of sand to the top of the mesa. There were a handful of tourists along with themselves, and an older Acoma woman who led them on the tour. Outside the various potter's houses, pots were on display, vivid in the dusty air, large and small pots, mostly white with black lines, some red and orange earth colored, geometric ware, beautiful shapes, like bodies or echoes of the hands that had shaped them.

The guide told them that every handful of earth for the graveyard and for the adobe church had been carried up on the backs of the enslaved residents. Therese wanted to put her hand in a fist and shout, but Mary was simply touched by the beauty of the church. She wanted to stroke it with her hand. Straw was visible in the adobe. Didn't the Jews in Egypt have to make bricks without straw, when they were slaves, conquered as Acoma had been, or were bricks without straw something in a fairy tale, like the one about spinning straw into gold? She couldn't remember.

In the hard-packed graveyard there were white crosses and plastic flowers. The surrounding wall was carved with peaks, soldiers to guard the dead. The church itself was vast, narrow, with a bright altar of a cheerful madonna, saints, and God coming out of the sky. Along the walls, beneath the stations of the cross, brilliant paintings contrasted with the whitewash: a rainbow encircling yellow corn, with birds perched on each rainbow. A sun and a moon hung over the altar, both with round open faces. Somehow the painting reminded Mary of the Flying Horses, the carousel of the Island, which was also painted with the double faces of the sun and the moon, with a winged horse flying over the rainbow, with a mermaid combing her hair and a merman surrounded by water. The church stood still in the desert's wheel.

Mary crossed herself with the holy water as she entered the church. Therese did not. The sisters had not had much formal religious training. Their mother might have sent them to church on Sundays, but their father hated religion — superstition, he said, superstitious lies. Matty, in an angry moment, had said that he believed in money instead of God. He retorted that he simply believed in himself and in his family.

As children, Therese and Cathy had gone through a stage of going to the Baptist Church. They'd become friends with their summer neighbors, a black family from Baltimore with two little girls, who had owned land on the Island ever since their great great grandmothers, freed slaves, had come up to hear the preaching of the Bible camps on the Bluffs, a century ago. But church was more the company of their friends, the picnics, the intensity of the preaching, hymn singing, and amening than any real attachment to religion. Now, Therese was an atheist, Cathy a social church-going Episcopalian, and Elizabeth was considering converting to Judaism because of Jed. Only Mary was filled with some unspecific, barely articulate, yearning.

Above the door leading out of the church there was a red-faced sun. And stepping out the door there was a sudden exhilarating barren landscape, all high and blue and jagged. And snow, snow was falling, crystal, each flake seeming more brilliant in the brilliant air.

As the afternoon wore on, they headed toward Gallup, Mary driving, Therese half asleep over the map. The snow stopped as they lost altitude, and the sunset illuminated the red wall of cliffs. Gallup, New Mexico, was hideous, with

84

huge refineries and a city that was no more than a neon strip, a violent intrusion on the landscape. Still, Therese had reserved them a nice room in a motel, with all the luxuries. "What is this costing?" Mary fretted.

Therese just smiled. "Don't worry! It's worth it, don't you think? Isn't New Mexico amazing? Wasn't today fantastic? Did you like Acoma?"

"It was incredible . . . the best . . . Therese, you're wonderful. This is wonderful. Even this dinner is wonderful."

They were eating steak sandwiches in the motel dining room; out of Lu's sight, Therese reverted to red meat. The sisters seemed to be the only women in the motel who weren't clad in green polyester pant suits, and indeed they were also the only women there alone, without men or children. And yet they were happy, quite happy, with themselves and each other. Once back in the room, Mary put down a bath towel on the floor and did some yoga stretches, and then some silent meditation, which she had adapted from one of the books she was perpetually reading that said one could meditate on a mantra, a circle of blue flowers, the moon reflected in a bowl of water, or on the breath. Lacking other props, Mary was concentrating on her breath, counting in and out, in and out. Lying on the bed near her, Therese was having an anxiety attack, in which she imagined Lu going to California without her, Lu in bed with various voluptuous women, Therese sitting alone in a cold and dark apartment and finally putting her head in the oven and ending it all.

"Mary?"

"Shh. I'm meditating (in, out, in, out). Why don't you take the first bath?"

"Mary?"

"Oh, what?"

"I'm having an anxiety attack about Lu going away to medical school."

"Therese, I'm going to meditate for twenty minutes. Why don't you worry for twenty minutes and then we'll talk."

This seemed reasonable, but after a full five minutes Therese ran out of her desire to worry. Instead, she did take a bath, steaming up the bathroom until Mary demanded her turn.

The next morning they got up early and headed in the direction of Canyon de Chelly. The weather promised to be fair; the brilliant sky seemed higher than usual. They passed through barren land, high plateau, long plains. When they first crossed over into Arizona, pines were casting shadows on patches of new snow and the wind smelled of pitch and cold. There was a little motel on the rim of the canyon, exactly as the guidebooks had promised. For dinner, there was some kind of Indian or Mexican food, lots of beans and things wrapped in corn husks. They slept in the mysterious air, and awoke early again.

Canyon de Chelly was red cliff, cut down by the river. A narrow strip of green cottonwoods grew along the water, and the canyon held green fields within itself as well, fields that would be greener in spring. In high yellow boots the sisters stood in the mud and shallows finally fording the river. On the other side lay the ancient ruins, the cliff dwellings, houses of mud and stone set in the rock. One of the houses was still washed white. Therese sat on a fallen tree, absorbing the ruin, playing with a stone, listening to the river.

Suddenly, Mary sat down on the ground. She patted the earth absently with one hand and looked up at the cliff, the earth houses like worn faces regarding her through narrow window eyes. Then, everything stopped, all motion, the spinning globe, time; the air was crystal and frozen and yet everything was whirling through space at a tremendous speed, the ruined house, the women, the green cottonwoods, the flowing river. Did her heart stop? No, the blood was pulsing, pushing through the network of arteries and veins, and the river made its loud music over stones. An instant passed; everything was the same, everything was different. Then, they crossed back over the river.

On the other side, they met a herd of goats and sheep with tinkling bells. A child dressed in blue rode by, herding. Bits of wool were caught like snow in thorny trees. Shadows covered the canyon as light faded. Venus rose, and Jupiter with Mars, bright planets in alignment. Short of breath in the thin high air they hiked up slowly, back out of the canyon, home.

The next day, the sky lowered, threatening snow, the weather was thick, and the sisters were quiet, half in a dream. Going toward Mesa Verde, they drove on toward desert, past Shiprock, through the dusty town of Red Mesa, across badlands. They gained altitude again in hill country. Flurries of snow flew thicker and thicker as they climbed. The road turned white. The windshield wipers could barely move under the burden of snow. A white veil descended over the hills, the hairpin turns. The car, without snow tires, slipped suddenly, and Therese almost lost control as they lurched past a sheer precipice. Mary jolted forward, restrained by her seatbelt from crashing through the windshield. Therese, trained on New England roads, brought the car out of the skid without braking.

"Fuck," she said. "Fuck fuck fuck. That was too close, that one was. We could have been killed. Fuck fuck fuck." She turned the car around cautiously and headed toward Santa Fe.

That night Mary dreamed in slow motion that the car went off a cliff but that she could fly, although slowly and with great effort. In the morning Therese woke up not quite knowing where she was. She couldn't remember for a moment, then realized it was Santa Fe, in a nice adobe hotel on the main plaza. There was money left over from not going to Mesa Verde. Mesa Verde will always be there, she reassured herself. It's not going anywhere. Come back in the summer. But anything could happen. I might die. There could be a nuclear war. Lu and I could break up. Therese got up, drank a glass of water, and washed her face. Then she got back into bed next to her warm, gently breathing sister, and fell asleep again.

Both Mary and Therese liked Santa Fe, the square and cathedral, the adobe buildings, the Governor's Palace where Indian women from neighboring pueblos came to spread out their wares of pots and jewelry, sitting in their bright dresses in the sunshine that warmed the earthen walls. The whole town was like the bowls they had seen at Acoma, shaped gently by hand, lifted from the earth. Squatting next to one of the vendors, who sold silver and turquoise on a black velvet blanket, Therese bought Lu a brilliant strand of blue stones, and Mary bought herself a pair of hoop earrings, polished turquoise and silver. In one of the alleys that opened into a patio and arcade of small stores, Therese bought a large piñata shaped like a star and covered in gold sparkles, which kept shedding over everything. They found a cafe with strong coffee and delicate honeyed sopapillas, and sat there by the hour, warmed by the red tiled floor and bright murals of parrots and conquistadores on the walls. At one of the small round tables, they each wrote postcards to everyone they knew. After Canyon de Chelly and the snowstorm, it was reassuring to be back, as opposed to out, out in the center of vastness, where the desert and ruins and river were both moving and still. They didn't speak of the mysteries they had seen, the red sun over the door of the church, the bright planets over the canyon.

As their plane landed over the water at Logan Airport, straight into the Boston headwind, Therese remembered as she always did that Logan had a high percentage of fatal crashes. She looked at the skyline of Boston, the familiar outline of the Pru and the John Hancock building in the early cold dusk of the new year. Mary looked at the skyline too, and overcome by it all, began to cry. But Therese, being Therese, did not weep at all.

Chapter VII

The third of the largest towns, Oldtown, lies even further to the south and east, and forms the large heel of down-island. Oldtown was built by whaling captains, with upright white churches and grey frame houses, shuttered and fenced from their neighbors. Here is the Civil War Memorial park with its triangle of cannon balls, a former Baptist church now incongruously claimed by the Order of Masons, and the Congregationalists burying ground, with those most forlorn of grave markers that mark the empty graves of those lost at sea or dead on the South Sea islands. One stone shows a clipper ship at full rigging, while another bears the name of a certain sailor, victim of the Globe mutiny, who some say was eaten by cannibals. The epitaph of the town's only atheist reads: "By the force of vegetation I was brought to life and action. And when life and action cease, I shall return to the same source."

In the middle of main street in Oldtown there is a great tree, well over a hundred years old, brought back in a pot from China by a whaler or missionary who imagined that it would look nice in some Victorian parlor, next to the blue teacups from Japan and the fire-screen from India. But someone planted the tree outside, and it took root in the alien soil, branching and twisting until it was gnarled and gigantic, one of those trees whose roots reach down into the underworld and make a bed for the great sleeping serpent that coils in the center of things, and whose branches reach upward into the heavens, holding nesting birds, and then the sun, the moon, and stars. It bore no fruit, and no one knew what its name was. It looked like a ginko but was not a ginko. Japonica? Baobob? Balboa? Did it even have the name of a real tree? No one knew for sure.

Overlooking the Oldtown harbor, for like all the down-island towns it faces the water, is a memorial flagpole. The pole commemorates one of the few actions of the Revolutionary War to affect the Island. Hearing rumors of an approaching British ship, three patriots blew up the stars and stripes with some spare gunpowder to avoid the humiliation of capture. The patriots were three fourteen-year-old girls, whose names — two Pollys and one Maria — emblazon the memorial. Wild things, eager to blow something up, they were lucky to be on the winning side; centuries later they might have been women of the Weather Underground or simple punks.

A FTER THE BAR CLOSED, Mary stood counting her tips in piles of small change and flirting with the red-haired drummer. The band was a local one, with a consistent gig at the bar. They were passable but obviously not headed for the bigtime. Still, Mary liked the drummer, liked the way he played with an air of nonchalance, and liked the way he looked, well over six feet tall, dark red curly hair, skinny, a little raw-boned. Must have looked funny when he was a kid, but now he was quite handsome, with a soft southern accent, Georgia accent, which didn't hurt either. The thought of his wife and two little kids didn't dampen Mary's flirtation as it might some women's; rather the opposite. She didn't want to marry him, she wanted to screw him. She didn't really even want to talk to him, but talk is the usual preliminary to screwing, so she accepted it. They were leaning toward each other across the bar and he was twisting a blonde strand of her hair around his index finger. But as they were murmuring cosy idiocies at one another, the phone rang.

"Mary, for you," said the bartender, handing her the phone.

"Yes?" She was surprised, as it was well after one o'clock in the morning.

"Mary?" said a choking voice.

"Yes?"

"This is Elizabeth. Can you come over? Right away? I'll pay for the cab."

"Elizabeth? What the hell is going on? Is everything all right? Jed? Our family?"

"Everybody's okay, nobody's dead. I'll explain when you get here. I need you to sleep here tonight. Take a cab, I'll . . ."

"Okay, okay."

"Family emergency?" asked the drummer. His kids were always getting the measles or chicken pox and his wife called at all hours.

"Yeah. I've got to get a cab. Can you walk me to the Square?"

"Sure," he said laconically, and took her elbow to guide her over the slippery sidewalk. The gesture almost brought tears to her eyes; it had been a long time. She smiled up at him, a little bemused, the cold stinging her throat and eyes. He signaled for a taxi, and then bent down and kissed her very hard and full on the mouth. She got into the cab and gave Elizabeth's address.

"Cold enough for you?" said the driver.

"Yeah, too cold."

"Supposed to be a big storm brewing up."

"More snow?"

"Tomorrow night, they say."

"More snow than where I'm from," said Mary.

"And where might that be, young lady?"

"Oh, the Island."

"A lovely place, I hear, but I've never seen it."

"Where are you from? Boston?"

"Why no. Falmouth, originally."

"Falmouth! And you've never crossed over to see the Island?"

"No." He chuckled. "Funny thing. Went into the army, then worked on the Cape Cod railroad, came to Boston, been driving a cab for over forty years."

"Don't you miss Falmouth? It's a nice town, I've always liked it."

"Yes. You know, my father was the lighthouse keeper there. Big storms like this one, quite a sight to see." He pulled up in front of Elizabeth's apartment on Massachusetts Avenue. Mary paid him, and overtipped him out of her change.

"Too cold to work," she grumbled.

"Too cold not to," he laughed. "Good night, now. A pleasure to meet you."

"Good night," she waved. The old man looked handsome with his thick white hair and bright teeth. He had the red cheeks of a fisherman or lighthouse keeper.

Mary rang Elizabeth's buzzer; the driver waited until she was safely inside. Elizabeth and Jed lived in one of those venerable grey apartment buildings, with a courtyard and high ceilings, walls thick enough to screen out some of the street noise, but still not well insulated enough to protect from the heat of summer or the cold of winter. Elizabeth greeted her at the door, dressed in a pair of black lace bikini underpants and a large shapeless grey sweatshirt. Her eyes were puffy from crying and she was clinging to the phone's extension cord as if it were a lifesaver; she was speaking rapidly into the receiver, apparently to Jed. She gestured helplessly for Mary to sit down, which was not as straightforward a proposition as it might seem.

Elizabeth and Jed's apartment was basically quite presentable, with a spacious bedroom and living room, a tiny kitchen and equally tiny eating area, all with built-in glass cabinets, fresh white walls, lots of windows. The odd angles of the rooms, making it a series of parallelograms, pointed to a subdivision far in the past. The apartment was peculiarly furnished, however; the living room was dominated by half a dozen gigantic potted plants that were almost real trees, and by a raised sitting area that served as a large couch, with piles of pillows on it, in reds and purples. Fabric batiked with jungle scenes was stapled to one wall, creating a mural. On the opposite wall was a large Polynesian hanging, made of crushed bark; this, Mary believed, had actually been stolen from the Peabody Museum's basement by an old roommate of Elizabeth's who had been a graduate student in anthropology.

As the dining nook had been turned into a study for Jed, who filled the china cabinets with his books, the bedroom was supposed to serve as Elizabeth's, and held a desk made of red formica and file cabinets, the only comfortable reading chair in the house, several framed photographs of Marilyn Monroe, a postcard of the John Singer Sargent painting, diplomas, two broken tensor lamps and one working model, along with the actual bedroom set: a foldout futon bed, with matching quilt, all decorated in a rainbow motif that spilled pleasingly from one pillow case to the next. In general, though, Elizabeth did most of her work, grading papers and writing her thesis, at her office at school. This was fortunate because the bedroom-cum-study was also decorated in masses of Elizabeth's laundry, mostly black underpants and good silk blouses dropped about in heaps, as well as piles of newspapers, bills, unanswered mail, catalogues, magazines, and lost papers. It was painfully clear from looking at the apartment that Jed was neat and Elizabeth messy, and that he attempted to keep the mess relegated to the bedroom. In contrast, the kitchen was spotless, but they rarely ate in, favoring the neighborhood Greek diner for breakfast, the croissant place near the Square for lunch, and take-out spicy Szechuan food for dinner.

At Elizabeth's gesture, Mary lay down in the middle of the living room rug, which was a beautiful Persian carpet, also red and purple, that had belonged to Jed's grandmother. She pulled off her snow boots and left them dripping in a corner next to the radiator. Then she lay back and closed her eyes, but only for a moment, as Elizabeth noisily set the phone down.

"Hi," said Elizabeth, in an odd, blank tone of voice.

"What in the world is . . ."

"Jed's sister just tried to kill herself. She's been acting very weird lately, although she was pretty much all right this fall. But recently she and I went shopping, going around to some of the secondhand clothes stores, trying to find some nice antique dresses. You know we all look good in those silk ones with the shoulder pads . . ."

"Yeah. Women were built like women in those days. There's room for my breasts in those old dresses."

"Well, anyway, we were in that nice shop on lower Mass. Ave., you know, the one with all the black leather jackets."

"Like the one I have from Joe?"

"Right. And anyway, Laurel goes in the back and finds an old red coat, made out of good wool, with a black velvet collar, and then she starts crying and says it smells like her mother used to smell when she was a little girl, and then she decides it is her mother's old coat, although later Jed says it isn't, and she has a fit and wants the store to give it to her for free, and then she does the same thing to an old housedress, kind of nice, actually, a blue and white print . . ."

"Remember housedresses? Matty hated them because they reminded her of her mother."

"Umm. I remember you bought one at the Goodwill on the Bluffs and she went crazy, wouldn't let you wear it."

"Kept saying she hadn't left the slums to see her daughter dress like they were still living in one. And told me I looked like an Irish slut in it."

"Very nice. Anyway, Laurel tries to make off with this coat and housedress, the clerk is nice about it, and all, and seems to realize that Laurel isn't quite all there. So we leave, but that was the first sign I got that Laurel was on some kind of downward swing again."

"Do you remember," said Mary slowly, "those kind of straw hats dad used to wear in the summer? The ones Matty teased him about? Panama hats or something, with dark blue ribbons around the crown. Well, I might get kind of upset if I suddenly saw one that I thought had belonged to him. Didn't Matty give his clothes to the Goodwill? Maybe Laurel's father did the same thing?"

"No. He gave the clothes to the aunts. Besides, it's not the same thing. You might be sad if you saw a panama hat, but you wouldn't go crazy. Laurel is crazy. Certifiable. Psychotic."

"What else happened?" Mary wanted to know.

"She tried to kill herself. She just tried to kill herself. Not thinking what it would do to anyone, to Jed or her father, not even thinking what it would do to herself, she took an entire bottle of prescription sleeping pills, five Quaaludes, five black beauties, a dozen assorted downs, a package of anti-histamines, the remains of a bottle of codeine for a cough and washed the whole thing down with Tab."

"It sounds as if she knew what she was doing, as if she wanted to die. Isn't that the message? She was just trying to tell everyone that she wanted to die."

"Then why the hell does she call Jed, call him here, half a second after the last pill is swallowed, and tell him all about it, so she's rushed off to have her stomach pumped, which believe me is not pleasant?"

"Where is she?"

"They are all at Cambridge General; that's where the ambulance took her with Jed. He and his father are over there right now, trying to get her admitted to MacLeans."

"The private hospital?"

"Yeah. Private psychiatric. I'm not sure they'll commit her. Maybe she'll go in voluntarily."

"Wow. What a lot of pills. I'm surprised anyone could eat all those pills and live. Are you sure she took all that?"

"Dammit! I'm not a fucking doctor. How should I know. Leave me the fuck alone. I thought you came over to take care of me, not run a poison control on fucking Laurel. Sometimes I wish she would just die, if she wants to so badly, instead of dying by inches and taking it out on Jed and her father."

"Elizabeth!" Mary was set to scold, but then she saw that Elizabeth looked pale and green. Her hands were like sweaty ice, and when she tried to get up she staggered a bit. They both knew that Elizabeth was going to puke immediately; Mary looked around frantically for a waste basket or something, but Elizabeth made it, in seasick motion, into the bathroom.

"Get me a Coke," she said faintly, after she had finished vomiting. "There's one in the fridge."

"You're not pregnant or anything, are you?" asked Mary suspiciously, pouring the Coke into a glass for her.

"Jesus, no. It's just thinking about Laurel and those pills."

Mary almost asked: are you jealous? but stopped herself in time.

"I just want you to sleep here with me," said Elizabeth. "Would you? Would you sleep here with me? I mean, Jed will be out all night and probably take fucking Laurel over to their father's, if they can't get her into the hospital right away. Boy

95

the stepmother is going to be pretty upset, with all her little kids and all. Still, she's okay, the stepmother, I mean, and even fucking Laurel is okay when she's not overdosing or something." Elizabeth was sounding sleepy.

"Can I borrow this nightgown?"

"Sure." Then Elizabeth said in her very small, her smallest voice: "Thank you."

They slept late, well into the pale wintry day, but somehow it seemed easier to sleep once the sky had broken with light. They rushed down to the diner next to Elizabeth's apartment, because the "two eggs special, with toast and hash browns, juice, choice of tea or coffee" was only available until 11:30 A.M.

"So why is Laurel trying to kill herself? I thought she was in therapy or something," said Mary, trying to sound nonchalant, and deftly breaking the yolk of one of her eggs with her fork.

"She's so depressed, she says she has no reason to live. Frankly, I think that girl has undiagnosed anorexia. That girl hardly eats at all. Maybe that's even part of why she's so depressed. I really don't know. Jed thinks their mother's death hit her the hardest. She was still living at home at the time, in high school, and maybe somehow she felt responsible for it all, her mother wasting away and dying of cancer."

"Still, lots of people have parents who die, and they don't all try and kill themselves." They looked at each other obliquely.

"Yeah, like us, for example," said Elizabeth, bitterly, "I guess we were just raised to think life is a vale of tears and all that, and to not complain too much, although we seem to anyway. But at least we know we're better off here than our grandmothers were, sitting around in the potato famine eating thin gruel or something and dying in childbirth every minute and a half."

"It was our great grandmothers in the famine, I think."

"Oh well, whoever it was, at least we can be glad we're us and not them, if you know what I mean," she said, eating a forkful of the hash browns, which were really quite good.

"Jed's family were immigrants too, weren't they?"

"Uh huh. Jews from Russia. His grandparents came over around the first World War. The grandfathers were dodging the draft. I don't know, I don't understand it all. There's probably no sociological explanation. My theory is that when Jed's mother died Laurel felt totally abandoned, and Jed and his father bonded more tightly, which saved Jed, but that Laurel was still excluded."

"That sounds like it could be one of Therese's theories."

"Bitch!" said Elizabeth, but in an affectionate tone. "I just can't imagine taking all those pills. Even the thought of it grosses me out. I guess I just can't even imagine wanting to die."

"No?"

"No. Life just seems too wonderful to want to end it."

"I can imagine wanting to die," Mary said slowly. "In fact, sometimes I do want to die. It isn't exactly depression, more a sensation of exhaustion. Sometimes I just feel as if I can't go on."

Elizabeth burst into tears. "This isn't cheering me up," she said.

Mary bridled. "God damn. Here I am telling you something sad, something personal, and you want to be cheered up. You're so selfish!"

"Well, screw *you!* It's my almost sister-in-law who tried to kill herself and now you horn in on the act. Oh, Mary, when you talk like that, I think you're going to kill yourself too and leave me all alone."

"Oh, grow up. The whole world doesn't revolve around you."

"Bitch."

"Bitch." They began to laugh, until the waiter glared at them.

Elizabeth grandly swept up the check. "Time to go."

"Let's go to the museum again. Do you want to? It's free on Thursdays, and besides, it cheered us up the last time. Anyway, I'm too broke to go shopping."

Outside, the sky was grey and low, with a few snowflakes drifting down. The slush along the curbs was frozen. Sidewalks were treacherous with ice and piles of garbage. Mary absentmindedly walked in front of an approaching trolley, but Elizabeth yanked her back. Mary's heart accelerated, but she felt more disgust than fear. How was it that she found herself in such an ugly place?

The museum was unexpectedly crowded, and they realized that the Pompeii show was in town. Still, they had nothing better to do, so they got in line with the schoolchildren and suburban ladies in for a day of shopping. The show was advertised by a large photograph of a volcano erupting, red and vivid.

"This is supposed to cheer me up?" said Elizabeth, but she was smiling.

Mary was still thinking about how ugly Boston was, not all the time, but most particularly in February. She thought of the desert, of an adobe house with turquoise shutters and some kind of vine with purple flowers climbing over it. She thought of the Island, of looking out the door of the shack and seeing green scrub, white sand, blue ocean, bluer sky; and the gulls rose up in her mind's eye and the sandpipers scurrying before a wave. "It's so ugly here, how do we stand it?" she asked Elizabeth, but Elizabeth shook her head. She did not understand at all.

Instead, Elizabeth asked, "Remember, right after you had your abortion that time, Cathy and I took you to the movies to cheer you up, and there was that horrible scene where the woman dies in childbirth?"

"Oh, God yes, that was awful!"

"Well, the other day when I was talking about it in therapy . . ."

"Why are you in therapy?" asked Mary, interrupting suddenly, and for once candidly curious on this subject. Why you, Elizabeth, and not the rest of us? Are you secretly the crazy one? Did something terrible happen to you but not to us, something we don't know about? Why?

"Well . . ." Elizabeth hesitated. She didn't know how to answer without insulting Mary, or the rest of the family. She wanted to say: I'm in therapy not because of some terrible pain or trauma, but because of a gentle despair that permeated me, as I see it permeate you, sister. Not quite sadness, more a lethargy, a sensation of sleepwalking, of distance, of watching my own life as if it were a moving picture on the screen. I want more from this life than I was led to believe I had the right to expect. We were raised to feel that doom might overtake us at any moment, if we overreached, went too far. I wanted therapy the same way I want art, literature, money, sex, love, nice clothes, interesting conversation. I want to expand, to fill the space I know can be mine.

But Elizabeth could not say these things, standing on line for the Pompeii exhibit with her eldest sister. She could have told all this to Jed, but she didn't need to, for Jed understood. Sometimes she thought no one else in the whole family ever sat down to simply think about things, to read a book, look out the window and mull; they were reactors, actors, not introspectors. She imagined the night table next to her bed, on it was a copy of the second volume of Proust, a pot of flowering hyacinths, and an unfortunate half-eaten fudge brownie. Then she tried to imagine Matty's night table. She was so engrossed that she mused aloud.

"What do you think is on Matty's night table?"

Mary was startled, was this some kind of answer or was Elizabeth being peculiar and changing the subject? "Matty's night table?" she repeated, sounding stupid.

"On Matty's table I imagine there is a copy of the Sunday real estate section, a jar of cold cream, and a shopping list that is several months old."

"No, I think she has a romantic historical novel with a scantily clad heroine on the cover and a champagne glass full of frozen orange juice."

"Maybe. What about Therese?" The conversation was turning into a riddle game.

"Oh, I know the real answer. You guess."

"A dildo and a copy of *The Female Eunuch*."

"Bitch! *The Mobil Travel Guide to Arizona*, a wrench, and a package of Ramen noodles. Lu's mother sends them odd care packages from Japantown in San Francisco."

"Weird, very weird. What's on your table?"

"Oh! Do me! What do you guess?"

"A True Romance comic book, some cocaine in a wad of tin foil, and a bottle of blue nail polish."

"Silly! A book called *How To Raise An Ox*, by a Zen guy, an empty M & M's wrapper, and some cocaine in a wad of tin foil."

"Guess what's on my table," said Elizabeth.

"A penis ring and copy of the bible in Latin."

"Close enough. What about Cathy?"

"People Magazine and a tube of KY jelly. All her bank statements from the last five years."

They laughed as the line moved forward, and they entered the exhibit together. The first thing to meet their eyes was just what they feared: a corpse, or rather the corpse image of a dog and a man, both curled under the force of their death. They had once been flesh, then hollows shaped like flesh in the ash, now casts of their former selves, of the space beneath the grey volcanic wastes. Mary shuddered, but Elizabeth felt calm. She'd always liked the look of Egyptian mummies and hadn't minded dissecting the frog in high school science.

"I want those," said Elizabeth, pointing to a pair of coral earrings, impossibly pink and long, lying in a glass case next to a string of gold and lapis beads. She wanted the pomade box of alabaster too, the small glazed figure of a monkey, the mirror polished to a sea sheen.

Mary wanted to live in the reconstructed room of a villa, with a floor of turquoise tile and leaping dolphins painted on the wall. She wanted to wake up on the hard elegant pallet of a bed bathed in sea light, beneath the shadow of mountains, and listen to the birds in the garden and smell the perfume of just opened flowers. Or, she wanted to live, finally, in the sea, to never sleep, to float all night on her back, looking at stars above and the stars of fish below.

They finished the exhibition and went to the ladies' room. The basement suite smelled of drying wool, radiator steam, old cologne. Once inside the booth, Mary was again hit with the irresistible desire to write on the wall, and pulled out the lipstick stub. But what would she write? A phrase from the Zen book she was reading haunted her. It was like a hook. She couldn't understand it but she couldn't forget it either: "The stone woman gives birth in the night." She didn't understand it, but she was convinced it applied to her, so she wrote it in large bold letters: STONE WOMAN GIVES BIRTH IN THE NIGHT. It looked like a newspaper headline, but she was satisfied.

When they left the museum, it was late afternoon and beginning to snow harder. Snow fell, thicker, whiter, more enveloping, as they waved goodbye and went their separate ways. Snow fell on Elizabeth as she met Jed coming into the apartment building, and she grabbed him, hard, and held him

100

before she would let him speak. Snow fell on Mary, who didn't have to work that night, and snow covered the tree outside her window and piled in drifts on her window sill as she curled up in bed pretending to read. Snow fell on Therese, leaving work early and on foot because of the snow, and snow fell and fell until Lu's cats' fur was wet and they left tiny footprints on the back porch and meowed piteously to be let in; and the snow snowed all through the night and filled up the paw prints, as if they had never existed. Snow fell over the Charles River. The river froze, and snow piled and drifted. Snow fell over Charles Street and Back Bay and blew into the overheated condo where Cathy and John slept naked in their big double bed, curled tightly together in one corner, and when they woke up in the morning they were freezing cold and snow was melting on their floor. Snow fell over the dome of the Christian Science church, and over the fountains of that plaza, and snow fell on the El and the tumbled-down burnt-out lots of the South End, where kitchen ovens tried to heat whole apartments, and landlords or Boston Gas had turned off the heat for nonpayment, and snow fell as the derelicts and winos and bag ladies slept in the alleys, dreaming of steam tunnels. And snow fell over the Atlantic and covered the Island. The deer and quail hid away in secret places. The scrub turned white. Snow did not fall over Matty, who was wintering in the Caribbean, but snow fell over the graves of her mother and father, of her grandmother and grandfather, over Bunker Hill Monument and the shipyards, over all the bridges of the city. The city was buried, utterly white and still.

In the morning, Elizabeth was so happy that she called everyone, even Therese, and said, "Oh! You've got to go out and look. Harvard Square is right out of *Anna Karenina*, piles of snow and people promenading up and down and bonfires in barrels — why, it looks just like Leningrad! I mean, St. Petersburgh, whatever. Come on! You've got to see it."

Chapter VIII

At the center of the Island the land slopes gently upward. A more fertile highland makes the only truly arable land and supports a few farms, vegetable gardens, grazing cows, and sheep. From a promontory one can see the sea to the south, across the acres of green fields and pond, a watered resting place at the end of summer for the Canadian geese, those peripatetic tourists, who also like to stop and take the Island's air.

Here is the town of West Beersheba, Beersheba proper being located somewhere in the Bible but not on any map of the Island, although for some inexplicable reason the town was always called West Beersheba and never Beersheba alone. This causes some confusion to visitors, but the residents are content, as they are with all the unspellable Indian names for every pond and knoll and the unpronounceable Old Testament names for every crossroad and dell. The town of West Beersheba consists primarily of a general store, which in the honored tradition of New England general stores presents a jumbled paradise to the needy shopper — everything from Spackle to frozen hot dogs, decorative refrigerator magnets made of shells, chicken wire, morose fresh produce, and sparkling packages of Twinkies, needles, thread, screws, magazines, flats of tomatoes, lettuce seedlings, artistic postcards of typical Island scenes, ancient paperback books, gardening tools, lighter fluid, flea collars, soup (both canned and fresh chowder served in styrofoam cups), a stamp machine, a pay phone, hot coffee, staple guns, alarm clocks, manure, suntan lotion, denim overalls, blue metal cups, and pre-printed NO TRESPASSING signs.

A BOWL OF SACHET sat on Cathy's night table and filled the bedroom with the scent of potpourri, cloves and crushed roses. Beside it was a copy of *The Lilac Fairy Book*, marked with a dry maple leaf, and the thin gold chain that she wore every day around her neck. She looked out at the sunny room with morning pleasure. Light marked squares on the parquet floor, and the sheets, carefully chosen and a hundred percent cotton, looked like a bed of wildflowers. She stretched all the way out like a cat, once, twice, and smiled. John always said her hair looked beautiful in the morning sunlight, so blonde. Well, John was gone to visit his mother for the weekend, but instead of missing him, she felt the luxury of thinking about him, not unmixed with the pleasure of having the house all to herself. All to herself until tonight, because then she was meeting her own mother's plane; Matty was visiting for the weekend.

Cathy looked around the room and smiled again. She was a romantic. It was obvious from the wicker furniture and from the prints on the wall: dreamy sea-light scenes of a woman getting out of bed and of a breakfast table set with shells and strawberries. Well, why shouldn't life seem rosy? She had every right to feel happy, and she didn't consider happiness slightly shameful, the way her sisters seemed to. She'd had her own bad time, trying to decide on a choice of career and feeling conflict over each interview, each choice. And then the stream of young men, each more presentable and less satisfying than the last, until she'd found John, as much of a romantic as she, a man of good faith and values, and, even she had to admit, a man of solid assets.

She opened the window and smelled the wind. Did she imagine it, or was there the smell of earth, of thaw, of crocuses even, and green leaves? Well, it was still the middle of March, and in New England anything might happen, and probably would. She remembered one winter when it had snowed in May, for goodness' sake, and all the trees crashed down under the unaccustomed weight of snow on their leaves. Well, that probably wouldn't happen this year. She padded across the room and wrapped herself up luxuriously in her purple velour robe. In the small kitchen, toasting bread and brewing herself imported coffee, she was hit by happiness as forcefully as if it were a physical wave. Calm down, she said to herself almost severely. It was all right to be content, self-satisfied, but such raw happiness was a dangerous intoxicant, perhaps even addictive, like whiskey or morphine. Too much of anything was dangerous, she concluded, although perhaps money was the exception to this rule.

She spent her morning in a half-daze, happily vacuuming the apartment and scrubbing the bathroom, complimenting herself on her housewifely qualities, much as she knew it would drive her crazy to be one full-time. She went out shopping along Charles Street, and the neighborhood seemed to reflect her mood. Each little gourmet store looked more polished and appealing then the last, and the tips of the trees seemed about to bloom. By now, her continued happiness puzzled her. She didn't usually feel this way, so continuously happy, but at work she was busy concentrating on the rows of numbers in front of her, the ringing telephone, the office gossip outside her door, the latest turn of power politics, and even on her makeup, her plans with John for the evening. Today was special. She felt the warming sun; maybe it was love, or having a good life, or maybe she was looking forward to seeing her mother. Really, she couldn't explain it.

Then in the late afternoon Elizabeth called her, and happiness evaporated at the mention of their upcoming weddings.

"I have to get married on the July 4th weekend," whined Elizabeth. "I just have to. It would be perfect because when Jed asked me to marry him that time and I didn't think he was serious I flippantly told him I would marry him by the 4th of July . . ." This rosy emotionalism was unusual for Elizabeth, Cathy knew it could disintegrate into a more reassuringly characteristic bitchiness in moments if crossed.

Cathy held the canary-colored phone away from her ear. She had heard Elizabeth tell the story of her courtship a dozen times before. Then, unable to contain herself any more, she blurted ferociously into the receiver: "Look Elizabeth, I've been engaged for two years. I don't want to get married in June; it's a cliché. May doesn't give us enough time to plan. I want to get married on the July 4th weekend."

"Don't be so selfish. This is really important to me. Don't screw it up for me by being selfish; it's not fair."

"Don't *you* be selfish, for once, Elizabeth. Christ! I've been engaged twice as long as you have. Stop trying to upstage me. You're just uptight that your little sister is getting married before you. You want to steal all the glory away from me and it's not fair, it just isn't fair, and I'm sure Matty would agree with me if we told her."

"You're such a baby, always dragging Matty into everything . . ."

"Elizabeth! Please . . ."

"You're such a baby and you've always wanted to be the first to do something in our family, Don't take it out on me. I can't help it if July 4th is perfect for me and Jed. You'll just have to be flexible and stop playing the baby all the time."

"Stop it!" Cathy had started to cry. "I hate you," she said, and the sisters hung up their phones simultaneously.

Cathy stared down at her spotless kitchen table as if hypnotized, and wondered for the millionth time what was wrong with her sisters, wrong with all three of them. Well, for one thing, they didn't understand love, didn't know how to treat a man properly. Mary was completely blank on the subject. Had she really loved her husband at all? She seemed to be doing just fine without him. Cathy herself would be desolate without John. She probably wouldn't be able to get out of bed in the morning if he left her. No, she would be able to work, anyway, but she wasn't heartless. Marriage was important to her, she was not like Mary. And Elizabeth, who was making such a fuss. Could Elizabeth really settle down? She'd done nothing but flit from man to man, lover to lover; it was cheap in a way, emotionally cheap. And as for Therese, well, that was a stone best left unturned; Therese must hate and fear men. Well no, not exactly, she was hardly a virgin as far as men were concerned. Therese had had a stream of boyfriends in high school, all with motorcycles and beards. Then why was Therese a lesbian? Because Cathy's sisters were all crazy, crazy and useless, useless to her, not one of them had taught her how to begin to live. But she had learned anyway.

Late that afternoon Cathy drove to Logan Airport and met her mother's plane. At the gate she had a moment of anxiety. Would her mother really appear? And would she be the same, or would she be an old lady, the old lady they were all going to become, tottering toward death. Fifty-one wasn't all that old, really, but Cathy had lost her father and so she hovered over her mother a bit, the anxious baby of the family, afraid of orphanhood.

Then Matty came towards her, glowing in her tan and newly frosted hair, wearing coral linen and a necklace of blue stones.

"You're gorgeous!" Cathy exclaimed, kissing her forcefully.

"Thank you, darling." And then shivering, "God, but I'd forgotten how cold Boston is."

Cathy's apartment was warmly overheated as usual, however, and Matty relaxed, admired the view of the river, the vases of fresh anemones and freesia, the glass of white wine Cathy gave her. Her youngest daughter had done well for herself, no mistake about that. Matty felt temporarily lulled from her own worries, from her complaints about her daughters in general, in Cathy's presence. Lights had come on all over the city, and the bridges glittered across the river in arcs of light. Cathy bustled about proudly in front of her mother, fixing a dinner of gourmet items from the specialty stores: pate´, a whole roast chicken, cold pasta salad, Greek olives, French bread, raspberry tarts, hothouse pears. They delicately gorged themselves, exclaiming over the food and the details of each other's lives: clothes, weight, hair, money, men.

"Mother," said Cathy primly, "I really wish you were seeing someone, had a man friend or something. You're still young enough, and nice enough looking, don't you think . . ."

"Now Cathy, I appreciate your concern, but really, it's not quite . . ."

"I know, I know, not quite my place to be giving you suggestions about your love life. Still, Elizabeth and I were talking about it recently and she said she just couldn't understand why you weren't involved with someone."

"Frankly, it's just not that easy for a woman my age to find a man. Most of the men want someone younger. Look at poor Muriel's husband, starting a second family at his age."

"The children aren't his, and Jed was saying that . . ."

"In my case, it just isn't that easy. Oh I know you girls talk about me, but . . ."

Cathy had the sudden unmistakable intuition that her mother was not telling the truth. "You're seeing someone, aren't you? I can tell!"

"Cathy," said Matty severely, "can you keep something in confidence? From your sisters, I mean, and not repeat what I'm telling you?"

"Why of course! Tell me."

"Darling, . . . I do have a man friend. Well, that's not exactly it. I had a man friend, I mean I had two man friends, down in the islands. But now things have come to quite a pass."

"What?"

"Well, you see, last winter, I had a lovely time with this gentleman who is from California who winters in the islands."

"An affair!"

"If you like. He wanted to marry me, but somehow, well, it just didn't seem right. At first I thought I just wasn't over your father's death . . ."

"Oh, mama . . ."

"Then I wondered if perhaps there wasn't incompatibility on some deeper level. And this winter when we met again he told me he was engaged last fall, engaged to a much younger woman. I saw her picture, she is quite lovely looking, if cold. He said he would still like to continue seeing me . . . but of course I couldn't . . . I didn't even want to. So I cut the whole thing off . . . And then . . ."

"But mother, couldn't you have won him back?"

"I didn't care to. There was something, well, something not quite fine or honest about him. I think your John is a fine young man," she added abruptly.

"I do too, but why don't you keep telling me what happened."

"Well, I met another . . . man. I met him at the marina because I was interested in renting a sailboat and he is a friend of the owner, and we began talking and one thing led to another. He is not quite as eligible as the California gentleman. Not rich, although he does own some boats, charters and fishing, that sort of thing. A real sailor! Not particularly handsome but . . . clean-looking. A nice, nice face, grey blonde hair . . . younger than me." She giggled.

"Mother, how young!"

"Fifty."

"Oh, that's nothing. Go on."

"Well, I think I've fallen in love." Matty toyed nervously with her wedding band.

"How wonderful! Here, have some more raspberry tart. Isn't it delicious? Love! Well, will you marry him?"

"But darling, he's poor. Suppose he's just after me for my money?"

"Does he seem that way?" Cathy felt suddenly eager to marry Matty off, the way a mother might feel about a nubile daughter.

"No. Actually, he likes to live simply. Our idea of a date was for him to bring over fresh fish to barbecue, and some wine. We'd sit out and watch the sun set or walk on the beach. Sometimes go to a movie or a show. And he was so kind, good manners, best of all, kind. I even met his sons, nice young men, in the restaurant business."

"He's divorced?"

"Widowed. Eight years ago."

"Better still. He hardly sounds destitute, mother, what with his boats and some sons in the restaurant business."

"Well, they do own a hotel and two family-style fish places. But he's proud, I just worry . . . "

"Don't."

"Well, my dear, I guess you'll have a chance to judge for yourself. He's coming to visit me this spring. He's from New Hampshire originally; we thought we might sail a bit if the weather is passable, and maybe travel."

"Mother, this all sounds just wonderful. I'm happy for you, really I am."

"Oh dear, it's just that I'm so anxious about everything. I feel as if I was in high school again, before I met your father." She wiped her eyes with her hand, although she wasn't quite crying.

Cathy kissed her gently, and began to clear the table. "Chinese checkers?" she offered. "Maybe that will help."

Matty laughed. It was an old secret vice between them, Chinese checkers. Everyone else in the family had always teased them mercilessly for their delight in this foolish game. Like all families who live the entire year at the beach they had a host of diversions for rainy weekends, winter nights, summer storms: charades, monopoly, checkers, parchesi, backgammon, hearts, War, knitting, crocheting, Twenty Questions, riddles, bickering, quibbling, cheating, and squabbling. But only Matty and Cathy loved Chinese checkers; they loved its simplemindedness, its symmetry, and most of all, they loved its marbles. John refused to play with Cathy, maligning her favorite as childish and simple-minded, but she had saved the board to tempt her mother.

Matty chose the rich purple marbles, with swirls deep in their hearts; Cathy picked her favorite set, the small black ones. Cathy lost the first game to her mother. Towards the end of the second game, which Cathy was winning, she got up to put on some hot water for coffee. It was then that they saw the ghost.

He hesitated just before the kitchen door, the darkened hallway behind him. Al's wife and youngest daughter both stood very still, looking at him expectantly. He seemed to want to come in, and yet afraid to leave the comfort of the dark. The ghost Al looked young and rather natty, wearing a light summer suit in the style of the forties, despite the wintry weather. He had on a thin red tie and a straw Fedora. Between the three of them, husband, wife, and child, they did not breathe one breath. Then Al gently tipped his hat. He looked as if he might actually speak, and both women leaned toward him with almost imperceptible eagerness. But he only lifted one hand and waved, either in greeting or farewell, turned around, and disappeared down the hall. He was gone, and they didn't attempt to follow.

"He always did like that jacket," mused Matty. "I'm surprised he still has it. He was one for saving things, clothes especially. I guess you wouldn't remember the suit. He had it before you girls were born."

"I love him," said Cathy. She had considered reacting to the situation by going to pieces, but decided against it. "I love him a lot and I really miss him. I wish he could come back, you know, be alive again. I wish I was little and could sit on his lap. That always made me feel so safe." She felt as if she was going to cry; embarrassed, she began fooling with the coffee maker.

"Do you believe in ghosts?" she asked Matty.

"No," said her mother. "But I'm glad to see everyone looking so well. Your father looked quite handsome and even Muriel looked much better . . ."

"What?"

"Oh, nothing, dear. What were we talking about? Is the coffee ready?"

"Yes, I'll bring you a cup. No, sit down. I'll get the cream, too." Cathy felt queasy from the emotional experience of seeing her father, but she also felt smug. No doubt her sisters had never seen a ghost. No doubt Al appeared in her kitchen because she was his favorite, his baby. She didn't think she was going to mention any of this to her sisters, much as she would have liked to lord it over them.

Matty showed no inclination to discuss the ghost further, and although she gracefully lost the second game of Chinese checkers, she mercilessly beat Cathy at the third. "I should call your sisters," she said, yawning, "but I'm just too tired tonight, traveling and all the excitement tonight. I'll call them in the morning. How is everyone?"

"Oh, they're fine," said Cathy. "Elizabeth is bullying me about the wedding dates but everyone else is okay. Therese looks great, as always, although her clothes are still a wreck. I don't know why she doesn't pay more attention to her appearance, she's so good-looking to begin with."

"Mary still working at the club?"

"Yes, until summer I guess." They both yawned, and Cathy made up the couch for her mother.

The night was cold and clear, midnight by the clocks of the towers. Cathy and Matty slept in their separate dreams. Jed and Elizabeth were walking down Massachusetts Avenue, going home after a double feature, holding each other's mittened hands. Therese and Lu were taking a hot bath together and shampooing each other's hair, bickering and flirting as foreplay. Later, as the bar was closing after last call, Mary sat on a high stool counting her tips. As she'd expected, the red-haired drummer took her by the hand and led her out into the back alley. It was deserted, and cold; their breath hung steam in the air. They started kissing hard, and he lifted her against the wall and began to fuck her; she was standing almost on tiptoes and one of her legs was wrapped around him. With intuitive foresight Mary had taken off her underpants in the ladies' room; at the same time she'd put in her diaphragm, but it still annoyed her that he hadn't thought to ask if she was protected. And wasn't he worried about getting a disease? Still, he was a family man, a safe health bet. And it felt fine, felt wonderful really, to be warm in the cold air, and kissing a man whose mouth tasted of cold and smoke.

"It's freezing!" she said, when they were done. Then she laughed, it amused her to think that she'd been doing it only a few feet away from the traffic on Mass. Ave. An almost warm breeze blew off the river and smelled wetly and piercingly of spring.

"Hi there," said the drummer, and kissed her once again. "This was fun. We should do it again sometime. Can we get together? I mean, our gig here is over. We'll be playing out in Braintree from now on, but I would like to keep on seeing you."

"No, I don't think so," she said. "I'm sorry, but you see, I'm planning to go home soon. To the Island."

Mary went home and slept like the dead. Her feet were killing her and she dreamed about shoes. Matty awoke to Cathy's sunshine, and caught a small plane back to the Island, vowing to call her other daughters as soon as she was settled in and had opened the house properly. Cathy tidied up, read the entire Sunday paper, and caught a case of the late afternoon Sunday blues. By then, she was ready to work herself up into a fit over her quarrel with Elizabeth. As soon as John walked in the door she poured the whole story out to him, exactly as she had promised herself she wouldn't do in just the tone that she most despised herself for using.

"Oh, honey," he said, "it's not that bad."

"But it is. She wants to get married exactly the same time that we want to get married. She's trying to upstage me. She can't bear for me to do anything first. She's being all nasty and jealous about it and making me wretched."

"Do we have to go into this right now? I'm exhausted, the train is such a drag . . . and you know my mother." He sounded peevish.

"How is your mother?" she said, suddenly contrite.

She bit her fingernail, the one on the ring finger of her left hand, and listened as he ran the water in the bathroom. Now he was mad at her, and probably didn't even really want to marry her. Life was wretched, and she was impossibly alone. John came back into the kitchen. All he really wanted from life right now was a beer and a sandwich, and yet he doubted the possibility of either. By the light of the refrigerator, Cathy noticed again how handsome he looked, standing there shirtless, with a damp towel around his neck. Well, now that he was back, at least there would be hot dinners again. He was a good cook even if he didn't love her. She couldn't cook at all. At least she was a good shopper. No rotten apples, no brown lettuce, no imperfect piece of produce ever found its way into her shopping cart, let alone her refrigerator. She owed that to Matty, who loved fruits and vegetables as if they were children, who considered spoiled produce a sin against God and humanity, a blight on the family honor.

"This looks great," said John, smiling into the contents of the refrigerator: dark beer, two bottles of Guiness, Italian salami, liverwurst, perfect tomatoes, herbed mayonnaise, Jewish rye bread, and Pommeroy mustard. "It's a good thing you can afford to shop, because you sure can't cook!" He grinned as he constructed an enormous sandwich.

"John . . ."

"Yes, sweets."

"I'm still upset about Elizabeth."

"Sometimes I think you only love me because I protect you from your sisters."

"Do you love me?"

"I love you."

"I love you too."

"Good. Now that that's settled, why don't we elope?" he said.

113

"Don't be silly."

"What's silly? Here I am asking you to marry me and you accuse me of being silly. Woman! I'm serious, why don't we elope? You didn't want a big church wedding anyway, did you?"

"Well no, just a nice garden party at my mother's or something."

"So we'll elope and then your mother can give us a party later."

"Maybe. Maybe it's not such as bad idea. Maybe you're right. Wouldn't that show Elizabeth! No, the whole thing is too crazy."

"Not crazy at all. We just get the blood test, go down to city hall, get married, come home, make wild passionate love to consummate the thing, call everybody and tell them, and then wait for the presents to roll in."

She giggled. "You're insane. Okay."

"Okay what? You mean you'll do it?"

"Sure. But what will I wear?"

"Oh, get something nice. You have good taste; suit yourself. I'll buy you flowers."

Suddenly they were beaming at each other, two idiots side by side at the kitchen table. Cathy could almost begin to imagine the scene, the two of them at City Hall, John with a white carnation in his buttonhole, she in a pale silky dress, something romantic but understated, maybe a hat, the two of them hand in hand walking down the long flight of steps, married at last, forever, a light snow falling or maybe a few early crocuses poking through the earth, purple and gold. Everything was going to be all right.

Chapter IX

West Beersheba also contains a gas pump, and the agricultural hall that houses the annual county fair. During the fair, West Beersheba suddenly becomes a site of importance, a center of activity and being. The fair! Only a few acres, but with all the right smells of popcorn and dust. Here are the winners of contests, the blue ribbons for beach plum jelly, the first prize for an apple-rhubarb pie. There is an oxen-pulling contest, suspenseful as it is slow, and a show of the heavy, gentle work horses. And best of all, there is the ferris wheel, that great circle of lights that lifts its wide-eyed passengers high into the balmy air above the center of the Island, a stomach-churning high, so high that the fair beneath looks like a doll's set, so high that one can see the sea off South Beach and even, perhaps, see one's own house, tiny and invitingly familiar, miles away, lit up and beckoning in the falling dusk.

115

"**C**ATHY HAS ELOPED!" shrieked Elizabeth, directly into the telephone.

The revelation hurt Mary's eardrum, but not her sense of order. "Oh, that's good," she said, a bit too vaguely for Elizabeth's satisfaction. Perversely, Elizabeth was the first person that Cathy had called about the happy event.

"What do you think?" she demanded.

"Think? What is there to think? It's nice. Probably they just wanted to get the whole thing over with, without a lot of fuss. I'm sure a lot of people feel that way, and Cathy and John actually did something about it. Really, it seems quite romantic and daring for the two of them, don't you think?"

"I think Cathy was trying to upstage me," said Elizabeth. She sounded peevish even to her own ears.

"Oh, come off it. I think you're exaggerating."

"Don't invalidate my feelings!" said Elizabeth sharply. Mary was sure she had picked up this peculiar phrase from therapy. They were at the conversational juncture where they might profitably fight, call each other a bitch, and slam down the phone. Mary inclined to a different tack. Perhaps it was the sweet April air, perhaps it was that although she had suddenly turned thirty she had not died or become peculiar-looking, perhaps it was simply that she was leaving Boston and the club in three weeks and going back to the Island. Whatever it was, she felt full of sweet breath, and an uncharacteristic pleasantness pervaded her manner with Elizabeth.

She said peaceably, "Shouldn't we do something for Cathy? I'm sure Matty will have a party, but maybe we should take her out, just the sisters. Can you think of a good place? You've got a much better sense of that sort of thing than I do. And don't be mad at Cathy. She hasn't upstaged you at all, because now you'll get to have the big wedding that everyone will remember."

Barely mollified, Elizabeth grunted: "The Copley Plaza."

"The Copley Plaza?"

"Yes, we could take her out for high tea there. The lobby is so elegant, and I'm sure Cathy will like it."

"It sounds perfect. Friday?"

"Friday."

"What shall I wear?"

"Oh, just something pretty. It's not that formal." Hanging up, Elizabeth felt as if she had spent her entire life talking to one or another of her sisters on the phone. The phone was their umbilical cord with each other, nourishing and sustaining, but at times it also felt like a spider's web, sticky and fatal.

On Friday, Elizabeth left herself plenty of time after her last conference with a student to change and take the T to Copley Square. Mary was free until the evening, but Cathy and Therese each left work early to make the five o'clock date. But in the late afternoon a gigantic train tank car was derailed near the Lechmere depot, releasing a cloud of toxic gas into the air. The surrounding neighborhoods were evacuated, and minor panic set in among the residents of Boston and Cambridge.

When Lu, who was home cooking, heard the news on the radio she imagined a hideous green cloud that burned everything it touched like some kind of cosmic scouring powder. Chlorine? Chloride? It was something like that, and probably right at that moment it was enveloping Therese, mutating her genes, giving her cancer, killing her cells. Of course Therese did not work anywhere near the accident, and at least she had her bicycle, which would be useful in the crush of traffic created by the poison gas panic.

Maybe Therese would call from the Plaza. Would she eventually come home for dinner? Would she even be hungry after all that tea? She had promised she would come and eat, Lu fretted. Of course, Therese was not actually due for another three hours or so, but Lu still worried. Her worry must be the sign of real love, she thought. She had never worried about anyone else before.

Lu set about slicing up the octopus she had bought at the tiny Japanese grocery store in Central Square. Although they were ostensibly vegetarians, Lu and Therese made an exception for sushi, so Lu planned the octopus for dinner, along with green mustard, ginger, and a cucumber salad.

Lu and Therese; they were an odd combination, thought Lu. She knew Therese did not entirely approve of her. It was not based on this whole med school thing. She had been lucky enough to get into UC Med and she knew she had convinced Therese to move with her, even if Therese wasn't quite ready to admit it yet. No, Therese disapproved of Lu herself. Her wild easy ways, her child-of-the-Berkeley-sixties manner, troubled the puritanical Therese.

Lu had grown up in Berkeley and gone to college there. She was the daughter of a fourth-generation Japanese mother and a father who was an ex-New Yorker. She'd been in the riots, and married a man at nineteen to keep him out of the draft. She had almost immediately fallen into the worst and most conventional roles of married life, the one who cooked and stayed home. Her history showed her to be a little older than Therese, who had spent most of the war in high school on the Island, driving around in too-fast cars with too-drunk boys, screwing on the beach. And even now Lu was the one at home, cooking and worrying. She had to laugh at herself, for unlike Therese she did not believe in conversion or redemption. She believed in herself as herself.

What shocked Therese about Lu included her marriage, which after the first year had been what was called in those days "open". Lu had even lived with her husband and another man for a while, but even in this arrangement she failed to get any attention other than the sexual kind. Then she had begun falling in love with women, in a heightened platonic way at first, and then with obvious lust, but it had been another three years before the last of the marriage had broken up. Lu's history bothered Therese.

"If I died," asked Therese, "do you think you might sleep with men again?"

"Sure, why not," said Lu, watching Therese grimace with distaste. For Therese, sex was dogmatic, ideological, but for Lu, it was a touch and a kiss.

And yet they had lived together with pleasure in each other for almost four years. Lu had explored and absorbed Therese's warm body and warm heart. And she had enjoyed her beauty, for Therese was certainly the prettiest in her family, tall and strong and golden-haired. She had made Lu feel it was safe to be kind, and for this Lu loved her.

Lu looked down at the remains of the octopus and apologized faintly in her mind, thanking the creature for being dinner. She often felt grateful to vegetables too, for they were also alive, and who was she to say that the carrots and cabbage didn't also protest when pulled from the earth. A few purplish tentacles remained, covered in suckers. Without ceremony she dropped them out of the window and into the alley behind the house, and was rewarded by the scurry and meow of cats.

Therese pedalled furiously through traffic, but knew she would be late anyway. She was dressed in a black turtleneck sweater, a pair of black jeans that were now strapped tightly to her ankles with bicycle guards, a pair of white sneakers that were unfortunately showing the dust of her journey, and a silky scarf printed with goldfish that she had borrowed surreptitiously from Lu. Perhaps not the usual wear for tea at the Plaza, but it would have to do. She, Therese, was quite simply Therese. That was all there was to it. And she wouldn't change an inch or an ounce of herself for anybody. The odd thing was, though, that she had somehow come to accept that she would go to San Francisco with Lu. They had not discussed it, and yet Lu seemed to know it too. Oh, the unconscious workings of the mind! Was this a hideous compromise for love? Did she love Lu? She assumed she did, but sometimes in the middle of the night she would roll over and see Lu and not know or particularly care who Lu was. Perhaps that was just sleepiness. Maybe you could never really know if you loved someone until much later, like until you were old or dead. Maybe what she felt for Lu wasn't true love, just some pleasant mixture of like and lust. But wasn't that love? Who knew? It would have to do. She was content. She would go to San Francisco. Therese pedalled harder.

As she had suspected, Elizabeth was three minutes early, and the first of the sisters to arrive at the Copley Plaza. She looked around the lobby with pleasure at the high, gilded ceiling, the smooth counters of marble, the dainty, uncomfortable seats of crushed velvet. She went off in search of the ladies' room, knowing that she was properly dressed for the occasion, and therefore, inconspicuous among the crowd. The ladies' room was also appropriately ornate, complete with a chaise lounge to lie down on if one had the vapors. Elizabeth went to pee in one of the stalls that was the size of her entire bathroom at home. Then she admired herself in the full-length mirror that covered one wall of the lounge. Would anyone looking at her know who she was? Or did she look delicate, pampered, a rich wife in for a day away from the suburbs? No, her expression was too fierce, and her hands gave her away: the nails were stubby, and she had ink stains on her right hand. She scrubbed her hands quickly with some ineffectual-looking but perfumed pink soap. Then she reapplied a bit of her pale lipstick and admired herself again. She did look fine, in a soft cotton shirtwaist in a Liberty of London print: real, and hideously expensive, even bought, as it was, on sale. The print was lavender flowers and pale green leaves; she was wearing mauve stockings and mauve sandals with short heels. Then, because it really was still too cold outside for such a dress, she had her mauve angora sweater draped over shoulders. She was wearing amethyst earrings, a present from Jed's father that had belonged to Jed's mother. And she was wearing her collection of gold bracelets and friendship rings that she never took off, even to wash or sleep. She smiled at herself. Was that a wrinkle, a laugh line? She grimaced. Then she smiled again. It didn't matter. Her dissertation was almost done. She had a job; she would get a better one. She would get married. Unlike Mary, she would not indulge in an orgy of contemplating her own mortality. Maybe she and Jed would have a baby, or two babies. Maybe they would buy a house and grow corn and tomatoes and zucchini in the backyard in the summer. Maybe she would try a different shade of lipstick. But first, she would have a large tea at the Copley Plaza with her sisters.

When Elizabeth made her way to the tearoom, open to the lobby, but decorously marked off by dividers of velvet rope, her sisters had still not arrived. She seated herself placidly at one of the round marble-topped tables with four chairs, murmured to the waitress, who was dressed in black with a white lace apron, that she was "waiting for someone," pulled out a middle volume of Proust and pretended to read it, all the while eavesdropping and observing the scene around her. Two well-dressed shoppers next to her were deep in conversation.

"And after the illegal abortion, which was just grisly . . . you know, she'd inserted a small twig . . ."

Elizabeth's ears perked up. Such an incongruous conversation for such conventional-looking women! But then she realized, with disappointment, that they were just discussing a new movie that Elizabeth had already seen and found facile, if literary.

Next, Elizabeth's interest fastened on a young woman, professionally dressed, briefcase in hand, waiting for someone, no doubt a man, for she kept running one hand through her short, stylishly cut hair. A lover? A husband who had reserved a room at the Plaza for an afternoon in bed between business meetings? Elizabeth made up a story that the woman was a divorce lawyer who had fallen in love with one of her clients. The briefcase contained a black lace crotchless teddy along with the final papers for his divorce. They would go upstairs, and . . . but Elizabeth's fantasy was cut short at the arrival of a squat middle-aged man with a bushy red beard. "Professor!" the woman cried, "We were so worried!" and then hurried him off to a conference room before Elizabeth could hear or invent more.

Mary arrived, ten minutes late, and looking windblown.

"Poison gas! The stupid poison gas made me late. I left in plenty of time to get here but the poison gas screwed everything up."

"Poison gas? What in the world are you talking about?" Elizabeth examined her sister critically for signs of insanity. She had always suspected that one day Mary would deepend it and go completely insane. In fact, Elizabeth suspected this of everyone in her immediate family except herself.

"The poison gas? You don't know? A huge railway car tipped over and released chlorine clouds all over everything. The whole north Cambridge area is closed, and the traffic is miserable, just miserable. We were advised not to travel unless it was an emergency, but I thought this was an emergency, and besides, I'm really in the mood for some pastry, so I just came over. That's why I'm late."

"Jed?"

"What about Jed?"

"What about Jed? I just wonder if he's all right. He could be dead or something. I'd better call." She began fumbling with her change purse.

"But Elizabeth, be sensible. He's at B.U. all day. He's not anywhere near the accident. And besides, no one is dead at all from this; there's just a lot of traffic. Anyway, you probably won't be able to get through, because half the phone circuits in the city are jammed with crazy wives trying to call their husbands."

"I'm not crazy, damn it. I just want to see if Jed is all right."

"I'm sure he's fine. Now why don't you sit down and tell me how you are. You look great. The dress is gorgeous. Did it cost a fortune?"

"Well, yes, thanks, but I got it on sale. You look . . . nice, too."

"Nice" was perhaps not the most adequate description of Mary's appearance, thought Elizabeth. She was dressed rather oddly, in a second-hand black and white silk print dress from the thirties. It did complement her full figure, and shoulder pads were an addition to anything, but Mary had rather ruined the effect by wearing a pair of ancient heavy leather boots and an equally scuffed, equally old, bulky, brown leather jacket.

"Yes, I got the dress at Esmeralda's," said Mary, "that secondhand clothing store near Central Square."

"Did you get the jacket there, too?" asked Elizabeth, feeling bitchy.

"No, it was Joe's. I used to wear it all the time on the Island, so I just borrowed it for the winter." She suddenly sounded tired.

"Do you miss him?"

"Yes. No. I didn't really like him by the time we split up, you know. Maybe I still loved him, but I just didn't like him any more. I used to try to talk to him toward the end, not about anything too profound, not like art or politics, but just about something ordinary, like surfing, and how it made me feel to be out there with the waves, not in control of the ocean but not out of control either, just with the waves, part of it. You know we used to surf right through the winter in our wet suits. Used to call that part of the bend 'Geezer's Point,' because all the surfers were over twenty-five, and we figured we'd still be surfing at eighty. Things weren't all bad with Joe, you know. We both love the ocean so much. We used to go fishing for hours off the breakwater at the bight. But after a while, he just didn't want to talk any more, not about surfing, not about sex, not about anything we'd had together. Sometimes I miss being married, just having somebody else there, a warm body, somebody who cares enough to ask how my day went, but mostly I'm relieved, not to be tied to someone, something, that was just so boring, finally boring."

"Maybe you'll meet somebody else," Elizabeth said tentatively. She was dying to know whether Mary had been seeing anyone, but Mary had been completely closed-mouthed about the whole topic.

"Well, you know, I did have a kind of an affair this winter."

"With who?"

"This guy at work, this red-haired drummer. He was really cute, but he was married and his kids always had the mumps or something, so it wasn't going to work out."

This didn't sound too promising to Elizabeth. "Better not get involved with married men," she said primly. "Any other possibilities?"

"Well, I'm going back to the Island at the end of the month, and you know how that is. The summer is just one gigantic pick-up scene."

"True, I was just wondering if you'd been seeing anyone else in Boston. You'd been so quiet about it, I couldn't tell what was going on."

"Well, yes, as a matter of fact there was somebody else. I was seeing a woman, but that didn't work out either."

"A woman! Who?"

"A woman in my group," she giggled. "But don't tell Therese."

"Was it fun?" demanded Elizabeth, more interested than shocked.

"Well, fun wasn't exactly the word for it. We were both kind of uptight about the whole thing. Interesting more than fun. Her name was Rania."

"Wasn't it awkward in the group? We're not supposed to get involved with anyone in my therapy group."

"It would have been, except she left the group."

"Did you tell them?"

"No, it seemed private. Besides, in the group we weren't doing therapy. It was consciousness raising or whatever you want to call it."

"What did you talk about? Your menstrual periods?"

"Don't be obnoxious. We started talking about our mothers, and sexuality, and stuff like that. But we ended up

123

talking about our class backgrounds, and about racism, and even about how we defined ourselves politically."

"Sounds heavy." Elizabeth was bored. She preferred hearing about sex.

"Well, it was good. I felt close to them, and I got to understand myself better. I just told the group that I'm moving back to the Island, and they were supportive, but it was kind of sad to think about never seeing them again."

"Did you say good-bye to Rania?"

"No. I don't even know where she is right now. And Elizabeth, please don't tell Therese or Cathy about my being with a woman. Therese will decide that I'm lesbian and try to bring me out of the closet and Cathy will decide that I'm a pervert and be afraid that I'll try to seduce her!"

At that moment Cathy arrived, frowning furiously from the effects of the traffic and the poison gas.

"What a day!" she exclaimed, hurling herself into one of the precariously narrow tearoom chairs.

Cathy waited for her sisters to comment on her appearance. It had been so difficult for her to choose what to wear that morning. John had teased her that her thin gold wedding ring should be enough, but she had been in a frenzy, trying on and discarding one outfit after the other. She could find nothing to wear that would both impress her sisters and still be appropriate for the long day at the bank. The grey suit with the cream was too wintry, the navy blue suit with the red bow was too straight for her sisters, and the more daring red dress with black blazer was too casual for the bank. John couldn't understand, no one could, how important her sisters' opinion was to her, not that they were particularly well dressed but more because of the way they scrutinized each other, with such criticism and such care. So she had done something a little insane, packed her small overnight bag and hid it under her desk at work, then changed in the ladies' room of the Copley Plaza out of the navy suit into the dress, a sleeveless wool, cut rather daringly, in a clear, pale red. She felt rather like Superman in his phone both, or Superwoman, transforming herself from proper banker by day, but into what? It wasn't as if she was meeting a man; why all the fuss? Was she a banker by day and a little sister by night, rather than a pure femme fatale? Was the only way she knew how to be a woman dependent upon her sisters?

Cathy's appearance, however, was a success, and Mary greeted her with a spontaneous gush of admiration: "You look gorgeous! That color! I've never seen you in it before. And the coral bracelets, they're beautiful too. Where did you get them?"

"I had Matty pick me out a pair when she went to the islands this winter. I gave her the money and told her what I wanted." The truth was that Matty had refused the money, but Cathy didn't mention they had been a gift. She was shy of her sisters' jealousies.

"I wish I'd though of that," said Elizabeth enviously, fingering the red coral on Cathy's wrist. "Shall we order? Therese is over a half hour late."

"It must be from the poison gas. The traffic is murder out there," said Cathy, hoping to excuse her own lateness as well.

"Oh God," said Elizabeth, putting her head down abjectly on the marble tabletop.

"Why, what is the matter?" said Mary.

"God, I just quit smoking, I've almost finished my dissertation, I'm trying to get myself together in therapy, and now all this happens, a cloud of poison gas envelopes Boston and Cambridge. We could be poisoned, we could be dying. Our lives aren't in our own hands. The environment is polluted, a nuclear holocaust could occur at any moment. Why do I try? Why don't I just go away to a tropical island and fuck and do drugs?"

Unfortunately, Therese was not there to counsel action, which was her therapy for despair. There was only Mary to take the philosophical view: "I think it is important to live life as you really want to, I mean, you could die at any minute, be hit by a car or get cancer, so maybe we should learn to live each day as if it was our last. If what you really want to do . . ."

Elizabeth peered at her bleakly. "We need some tea," Cathy announced in a brisk tone, signaling the waitress. "Four full teas, please, we're waiting for someone else, who should be here any minute. Thank you." Then she said to Elizabeth, "Maybe you've just got a case of the pre-wedding jitters."

125

"I've just gotten a cervical cap," said Elizabeth, changing the subject abruptly, as she sometimes did. Her sisters looked expectant. "It's great," she continued, "you can keep it in for days."

"Isn't it hard to fit?" asked Cathy.

"No, Dr. Stanley showed me how. You know, his caps were all impounded by customs because he was importing them from England, and the FDA didn't want them in this country, but he finally got them out."

"Oh, Dr. Stanley. I just love him," said Mary.

"He's too short," said Cathy.

"But he has a great beard," said Elizabeth.

Mary rhapsodized, "He's perfect. He's the only reason I don't want to move back to the Island. He always asks if you mind if someone watches the exam, and then when you say no, he brings in five medical students and the receptionist."

"And the receptionist practically gives you a breast exam when you come in."

"He cured my cystitis with cranberry juice."

"He saw me through the abortion," said Mary.

"He checks the diaphragm by having you get off the table and do deep knee bends."

"Maybe that's how he has sex!"

"He wears love beads."

"He does home births."

"Dr. Stanley is wonderful," said Elizabeth, "He's not a woman, but otherwise, he is perfect."

"Once, though," said Cathy, "he told me to put olive oil in my ears for the wax, but it didn't work."

"But that was because the olive oil was rancid," said Elizabeth.

The tea arrived in silver pots and on silver platters. There were scones with raspberry jam and butter, cucumber sandwiches, smoked salmon sandwiches, olive sandwiches, eclairs, napoleons, and cream puffs.

"I want to have a nice meal for once," said Cathy sternly to Mary, "so don't mention anything about food additives."

Looking up from the feast, they saw Therese coming toward them. Elizabeth looked from her sister to the sandwiches with satisfaction, for now they could begin. Cathy noticed that Therese was dressed like a cat burglar and carrying a bicycle chain, but she said nothing. And Mary got to her feet and waved frantically across the crowded tearoom and called: "Darling! At last! You're safe!"

Chapter X

Continuing up-island, west by southwest, is the small town of Beetlebung, which takes its unattractive and obscurely amusing name from a strand of trees at its center, trees used to manufacture beetlebungs for whaling ships, a beetlebung being a kind of barrel stopper and not an Egyptian scarab or the mythical dung beetle that pushes the sun across the sky. The town has only a hundred or so winter inhabitants, with ten times that in summer, and is marked on the road simply by the post office. It is a town of mailboxes, of stony scrub and beaches, a town of delicate stone walls, old stone walls, criss-crossing the woods and marking long-forgotten boundaries of field and property, lacy stone walls built without mortar, cobwebs against the flow of the rising or the setting sun.

Up-island is narrow, the light implies water on both sides of the road, the one lane that winds beneath the shelter of green trees arching low over it. The soil is too sandy to support much beyond scrub oak and pine, there are more animals than people: skunks, deer, badgers, raccoons, rabbits, otter, sand wasps, crickets, owls, crows, red-shouldered hawks, and the omnivorous gulls.

TWENTY YEARS AGO OR MORE, it was summer, and heat shimmered off the asphalt and popsicles melted or stained children's lips and tongues with purple or orange ice. New leaves covered the trees and the winged seeds of maples spun like tiny helicopters through the air. The world smelled like fresh-cut grass, dandelions grew on the lawn, and the fuzzy seed flew like wishes blown to the wind. At night, the stars poured through the sky in a thick milky stream over the cries of insects singing in the grass.

On the last day of school, the sisters ran through the house as if shot by a sling and then dashed out the back door and into the world of the backyards, and the further world of scrub, sand dune, the sea, oh the beautiful sea, that stretched like glass in motion all the way to China. After school, they wildly discarded the accoutrements of civilization: navy blue book bags, geography books wrapped neatly in map covers, Beatles cards, candy Pez in dispensers shaped like Popeye the Sailor Man, loafers slotted with pennies or dimes, Red Sox decals, and white ankle socks. They stripped off their grey pleated skirts or plaid dresses and hurtled into their bathing suits, red, white, and blue one-piece bathing suits with cute belts around the middle. Then, they flew out of the house and did not return until Labor Day.

At puberty, they were cast from Eden. They had to work in the store under their father's cautious eye and their mother's caustic tongue. Arranging vegetables, stocking shelves, ringing up the cash register and a thousand other tasks of the trade interfered with what the girls knew to be their real work: getting a perfect tan, fighting endlessly with their mother, losing their virginities on beds of pine needles and blankets of sand, weeping at the slightest provocation, taking insult at the members of their family, and talking on the telephone. But while they were still children they lived in paradise, each summer endless, each autumn unbelievable. That was the summer after the Cuban missile crisis, where they had hidden from bombs under their desks, but the bombs had not come and the world was still innocent of suffering. Then, their mother still had a few plates emblazoned with the heads of John and Jackie Kennedy. It was before the assassinations, before the war, before they knew there was a war, a war of any kind at all.

Then, they had lived for a full season eating huckleberries and onion grass, blueberries and stolen pies. Their knees were stained green and their fingers tasted perpetually of salt. That was when they had still lived in town, down-island, near the local supermarket that their parents were parlaying into a large luxurious one as they moved gingerly but surely up the middle-class ladder. The backyard was small and green; it had a swing set that their father had anchored with cement deep in the ground to prevent it from tipping over. Mary loved to swing, pumping herself higher and higher, until, with the vagaries of perspective, she seemed to be flying over the house, her feet bigger than the doors or windows. Two Memorial Day weekends in a row, Elizabeth had sat on the swing, looked up at its winter-ravaged chain, and gotten a piece of rust in her eye. Two years in a row she was taken to the emergency room by her father, who missed the parade. After that, he replaced the rusted chains with new, shiny ones each spring.

In those days, the girls knew that their father loved them, even though he was less present than their mother. He taught them to ride bicycles, removing the training wheels with great ceremony. And it was Al who taught them to swim, holding their hands to jump the waves with them, teaching them about riptides and undertows, cautious but unafraid. And when Mary began to surf as a young teenager it was he who encouraged her to save up her earnings for a board, and he who bought her a wet suit as an unlooked-for treat; and all this in clear defiance of Matty, for whom surfing meant either accidental death or a wild beach party, and she wasn't sure which was worse.

When they were still little, on rainy Sundays when the store was closed, their father would take them down to the Bluffs to the arcade. There, they could play Skee-Ball for prizes, a game at which Therese excelled, and she always won a stuffed animal or doll to carry home in glory. In the arcade there was also pinball, which Al loved but which bored the girls, except for Cathy, who liked to stand nose-high to the machine and watch her father manipulate the ball, hit the bells, flash the lights. It was a tribute to his careful attention toward his daughters that each of them regarded herself as his indisputable favorite. Each girl had mementos of those times: glossy black and white photographs, four for a quarter, showing her making wild faces while her father laughed and held her.

The greatest attraction of the Bluffs was the Flying Rings. The carousel, enclosed in its wooden tent, sported old-fashioned animals to ride: a long-necked giraffe, a cart drawn by elephants, a brilliant zebra, a horse with fiery nostrils. Like the menagerie of a circus traveling too long in north country, trapped by snow in the mountains, the animals of a tropical imagination wintered on the carousel as grey squalls blew in off the Atlantic. And so the little girls rode round and round, round and round, always grabbing for the golden ring that they sometimes caught for a free ride, and always found in their dreams.

Their neighborhood was one of soft grey houses, shingled, and white-fenced. Half-wild roses grew in the salty air, and black cats watched the milkman with an eager eye. Milk still came in bottles then, and broke dramatically when it froze in the winter or slipped out of eager hands and crashed resoundingly in glass and foam on the kitchen floor. In the summer, they drank chocolate milk with dinner, dark and sweet and cool, and went out into the infinite twilight to play with the neighbors. They played Spud until it was too dark to see the ball, and even then they would keep playing, although the kids had already been tagged out and gone to bed. They wore white nightgowns and slept in bunk beds, two to each tiny bedroom.

Beyond the world of backyards was the enormous world of sea and sky. Mary and Elizabeth longed for those blue spaces, and so they would take their bicycles and escape

132

together. At those times, Therese and Cathy simply ceased to exist. They were too small and their legs were too short. The biggest gap in age was between Elizabeth and Therese, almost two years, which should have made their relationship judicious, but instead made it distant. Elizabeth's bicycle was blue and had once been Mary's. It was named Melegar, for a mythical Irish steed. Mary's bicycle was red, and as it belonged to the privileged eldest it was new, and named Scarlet. They pedaled madly down the short driveway and into the long smooth street, through the neighborhood past the small houses, traditional grey-shingled ones and the newer Cape Cod-styled ones, the small yards dominated by vegetable gardens: tomatoes, cucumbers, lettuce, cabbage, carrots, radishes, and a few romantic waving rows of corn. They would bicycle dreamily on to the county road, up a few soft hills and down again, always keeping against the traffic as their father had instructed, even though that wasn't the law. They left the gardens behind and entered the woods, and then they might throw their bikes casually down on the pine needles and lie in the shade, dazed and cool, or look about for puffballs and Indian pipes, those pale, frightening fungi that pushed through dead leaves to glow with a greenish ghost light. In the spring and early summer there were ladies' slippers, real flowers with delicate pouches sprinkled in bloody speckles, a kind of wild orchid.

After the woods the sisters would continue on their way, the paved road slipping gently down toward the sea, the water barely hidden between low sand dunes and then emerging blue, the bluest thing in the world, over the ridge. That was before the Long Beach was flooded with tourists, the weekend trippers who stayed in the gingerbread guesthouses at the Bluffs and who lay all day in the sun trying to bake themselves into an object of envy at school or office.

Mary knew the names of all the beaches on the ocean side of the Island. White and shining, like a string of beads to tell, they formed the great Long Beach that ran the entire south side. The bay side of the Island was more convoluted, an intwisted series of coves that met the gentler water of the sound. Mary liked to say the names of beaches to herself quietly when she was frightened or sad: Red Cliff, Zach's Beach, Windy Gates, Hornblower's, Gull Beach, Stonewall,

Baldwin's Beach, Cranberry, Jungle Beach, Lucy's Beach, Crane's Neck, and eventually Long Beach itself.

The idea of sea level disturbed her as a child. Sometimes there were storms where the sea rose out of its basin and over its boundaries. Once, the high tide crashed over a seawall and crossed the highway, snatching a child out of a flooded house. After the storms, though, the tide lines were littered with mystery, beautiful and hideous. Mary found green sea urchins, old detergent bottles, tiny starfish, glassies, black skate egg pouches, stinking seaweed, whole fish spines, small sharks, and large lumpish skates. She would sing:

> *Cape Cod girls they have no combs;*
> *They comb their hair with codfish bones.*

But she didn't really dare to try.

Once a great hurricane had blown a tanker in so close to shore that it could not get safely out again. The boat sat out the storm, attempting to keep from foundering in the cove, and Mary had seen it. Like the moon, it looked so close she thought she could touch it. It was all lit up with strings of pink lights so that it looked like a pleasure yacht or an ocean liner.

One time, Mary had seen whales as well, a school of small black pilot whales, cavorting together in the warm summer waters brought north by the Gulf Stream. They were dancing and playing, not far off shore. For years she assumed she had dreamed them, until she described the dream to her fisherman husband, who assured her that what she had seen was typical of the whales.

Unlike the whales, her dream about the ocean was not comforting. In the dream, the sea looked somehow wrong, as if seen from below. It was trying to break over a jetty or was barely restrained by a fence or barbed wire. Often, for it was a recurring dream, she and Elizabeth were swimming together in it. Sometimes they had to run up the beach to try to escape a rising tide. Sometimes the ocean looked like prehistoric times, full of giant octopuses and armored fish that chased them, and the water was a peculiar green. But sometimes she could see shipwrecks far below, and the sea was beautiful. There were pearls and bright shells and once a whole display case of dime store earrings cast upon the shore for her to find. Then, she was sad to wake.

One quiet afternoon on Long Beach, Mary and Elizabeth had their first adult conversation with each other. Mary was twelve that summer, and Elizabeth a year younger. They were sitting in a sandy dell, a shady dipping down between two dunes, out of the sun. Elizabeth was drawing a picture in the sand of a moon-eyed lady with big dangling earrings, and Mary was idly making a chain out of tough beach grass.

"Do you believe in God?" said Elizabeth, apropos of nothing.

"Huh?" Mary wasn't thinking; she was simply enjoying being out of the sun. They'd been swimming, but even in her wet bathing suit, the sun was too hot this time of year on not yet tanned skin. It was June, and she was just beginning to adjust to the wildness of summer ways.

"Do you believe in God?" Elizabeth persisted.

"No."

"Oh," said Elizabeth, unable to keep the conversational ball in motion. She wrote in the sand with a twig "Elizabeth loves _____" and then hastily covered over the boy's name in case Mary should see it and tease her.

"Do you believe in God?" asked Mary, feeling philosophical.

"Yes," said Elizabeth.

"Do you pray?" asked Mary, torn between interest and scorn.

"Sometimes," she answered, a little defensively. "Like at night when I'm scared or before I have to take a test."

"Daddy says he doesn't believe in God."

"Uh huh."

"But I'm an agnostic," said Mary grandly.

"What's that?"

"It means you're not sure. Maybe there is a God, maybe there isn't . . . I mean, what if there was a God but you didn't believe in Him? Maybe He would be mad and come and get you. But what if there wasn't a God and you wasted a lot of time praying and going to church and then it turned out you were wrong, it would just be a big mistake. So it's best to be an agnostic, just in case."

"Oh," said Elizabeth, unconvinced. "But I like believing in God, even if there isn't one."

Mary watched the strands of beach grass throwing their delicate shadows on the smooth sand. Afternoon lengthened the shadows, and a cool breeze came in off the water. The quiet mood inspired Elizabeth, who continued volubly if tangentially:

"Are you going to have children? I am going to have four, but not like our family. Instead there will be two boys and two girls. A boy first. That's so the girl can have an older brother who will take her places and introduce her to all his friends so she can have boyfriends." This part of the fantasy was gleaned from *Teen* magazines rather from Island life, where older brothers tended to torment or ignore their younger sisters. "The oldest boy's name can be Robby," and here Elizabeth almost stammered, because this was the name of her secret love, the boy who sat in back of her in class. It was his name she had written in the sand, and it was him she had measured for a gum chain: an esoteric item, woven of multicolored gum wrappers, made to the exact height of the beloved object, and given as a token of romantic love from a girl to a boy. Elizabeth continued, "The girl's name is Jo," this of course from *Little Women*, a literary if masculine choice, "and then the next boy can be Alfred and the little girl can be April."

"But what if she isn't born in April?"

Elizabeth had obviously not considered this possibility. "Then I'll name her Pansy."

"Well," said Mary, "I will have three boys." It sounded like a relaxing change, after being the eldest of four girls. "I am going to name them for the angels: Michael, Raphael — you can call him Raph, and Gabriel — you can call him Gabe." She felt distinctly satisfied, as if the whole thing were duly settled.

That summer was also the summer that "it" happened. "It" was something that happened to Mary that she never told anyone about. "It" was more secret than getting her period, which happened the following summer, more strange than seeing the whales or her dreams of the sea. In fact, she rarely allowed herself to think about "it", but "it" was always there, like a smooth sea stone or a shiny ring hidden away in a pocket, darkened, but ready to be touched again.

That summer, for the first time, Mary would go off alone on her bicycle, feeling some obscure need to be only in her own company, without her sisters or either of her two best friends. She would sometimes make the journey alone to Berry Island, an isle that lay off the Oldtown harbor. To get to Berry she took the On Time Ferry, so called because it simply went back and forth all day between Oldtown and the smaller island. The On Time was big enough for two cars and a bicycle. The old grizzled guy who ran it always called Mary "Gorgeous," but in a way that made her happy instead of afraid. The channel was deep and narrow, the running tide made it dangerous to swim, and Mary had been warned against this numerous times. But once on the other side she had a sense of freedom, of adventure, although Berry hardly looked different from the Island she had left.

Berry was, in later years, made infamous by a sex scandal involving famous politicians. Its numerous coves and inlets also made it an ideal spot for a flourishing trade in smuggled cocaine. Movie stars and celebrities built houses on its secluded beaches, and it acquired a reputation of decadence and romance. But in those days it was quiet and unknown, with bright yellow beach cabanas on the bay side, giving it the look of nineteenth-century sea bathing, and the beach was littered with beautiful transparent silver and gold shells. Still, it had its mysteries, the great old houses sitting grey-shingled and white-shuttered, brooding over the harbor, summer houses that were impossible to heat in winter, where the furniture was draped in sheets. Cobwebs. Ghosts.

Mary would bicycle along the only main road on Berry, hitting her stride as the road curved away, sloping seaward. A short way off the road and into the woods was the most beautiful and mysterious place Mary had ever been. It was a garden, a secret garden, built by one of the summer people but out of sight of the houses. A curved wooden bridge crossed a small stream and led into the garden. Mary left her bicycle leaning up against a tree and slowly crossed the bridge. Sometimes she took off her sneakers and left them next to her bike so that she could enter the place barefoot. On the bridge, she wished she were dressed in something besides jean shorts and a T shirt. She wanted a kimono or a parasol painted with wisteria. After the bridge there was a wooden sign posted on a pine tree, carved with the words MOON GARDEN. The curved bridge was a moon bridge, and the garden was meant for viewing the moon. In a fairy tale, the moon might have lived here, sleeping in the daytime when she wasn't riding the night sky.

There were clumps of iris, purple and white, planted by the stream. The evergreens had been pruned into interesting twisted shapes; there was also a big rock with the sand raked in patterns around it so that it looked like an island rising out of the sea. Obviously, there was a gardener who came here to rake the sand and tidy up, for there were never any dead leaves in the garden. However, Mary had never seen anyone, although once she had noticed a broom lying forgotten against a tree.

By her next visit the broom was gone, but there was a new addition to the garden. Someone had hung a strand of glass wind chimes on a low branch. They made an intermittent, delicate, brittle sound in the breeze, like an insect song or the patter of water on stone. Mary froze, listening, her face turned up. It was unbearably perfect.

She stayed for an hour, sitting on a stone and breathing in the air. She never passed the garden without entering it if only for a moment, but her ultimate destination, today and always, was the sea. So she continued on her way, pedaling the length of Berry, which was not very arduous, and crossing an old bridge that was wide enough for one cautious vehicle at a time.

And there it was, the wide white strip of beach with the waves coming in one after the other, smooth and high. Swimming was dangerous here, for the sea floor gave way a few feet off shore and the shelf dropped off sharply into the undertow. Mary watched with satisfaction as a wave cut crosswise along another in the wind, and the backwash sprayed violently into the air. She walked along the flat shining beach, and sat down in the sand. Then it happened.

The sky was huge and white. It rang like a bell, and the world froze. It froze, but was moving too, and she was part of it. She saw the waves freeze and break and she froze and broke too. Everything was inside of her and she was inside of them. Then the world started to turn again at its normal rate, and she felt her legs tingling with pins and needles. She wanted to shout or cry, but she didn't quite know how, so instead she went home.

Later in high school, when everyone was talking about LSD, Mary thought that maybe it was the same thing she had known on the beach on Berry Island. But it wasn't, although the acid made colors move and hearts slip off a deck of playing cards and made her hands transparent and fascinating. She tried eating mushrooms, too, but they just made her nauseous and giggly. She couldn't find out about "it" in any book, and she never wanted to speak to anybody about it.

That summer, Matty was in an uneven temper, and Mary was often glad to escape on her bicycle. One interminable Sunday afternoon, when Al was out fishing and drinking with his cronies, Matty had asked the girls to clean up their rooms at least twenty times. Finally she threw a fit, and began yelling and screaming gathering up armfuls of their belongings and throwing them down the driveway.

"She's crazy," yelled Mary. "Get Daddy! Call the police."

Matty hurled a Beatles album out, where it cracked satisfyingly on the pavement. Therese and Cathy were rather enjoying the spectacle, until she slapped them roundly on their hands. Then they began to howl. But it was Elizabeth who was affected the most adversely by the scene. "It's unjust! It's unjust!" she wailed. Matty hit her too, but she hit Matty back and rushed out of the house and into the quiet street, where she sat sobbing on the neighbors' pavement until a sleek black cat came up to her and began purring and butting her hand with its head. Then she stopped crying, but she was unable to let go of her grudge: her mother was a tyrant, a witch, worse than the Russians or the Nazis. Most of all, Elizabeth felt the humiliation of having been punished along with her sisters, as if she were one of them, not herself, individual and inviolate.

However, at times all four of the sisters could play together in harmony. One of their favorite games was called "Being the Beatles," with Mary as John Lennon, down to Cathy, cursed with the inevitable fate of being Ringo. They would talk to each other in what they imagined was a convincing

Liverpool accent, and they would play the records loudly, playing along on air guitar and mimed drums.

Mary had also invented an adventure game call "Little Schoolhouse in the Blizzard." This game could only be played in summer, for it consisted of them cramming themselves in together under the picnic table in the backyard. There, sweltering in the heat, they would make up dialogue about how they were slowly freezing to death as the stove went out and the drifts of snow piled higher and higher against the prairie schoolhouse. Sometimes there were wolves, desperate gunmen, and once even an incongruous Martian princess, but the script was usually naturalistic. There they were, four sisters alone in the wide-wide world, without father or mother to save or blame them.

Chapter XI

At the far west end of the Island, on a boot-shaped peninsula, lies the last town of the Cliffs, as well as the actual cliffs themselves, great clay ones, multicolored and beautiful in all the tones of earth: red, white, brown, black, but slowly crumbling into the on-pressing sea. The cliffs are the place of sunset on the Island, where the sun sinks with quickening pace below the violet rim of the horizon, darkening the opposite sky into a velvety blue. If you watch closely, you can see a green flash across the sky at the exact moment that the sun sets.

The Cliffs is one of the only two Indian townships in the Commonwealth, and the residents were once famous harpooners. Now the head of the Cliffs is covered with concession stands, selling wind chimes, moccasins, and "Indian" beads made in Japan, along with sodas for the thirsty tourists. But even here are those, Indian and non-Indian, who watch the Island and guard it from harm, solitary walkers and beachcombers, who, with their presence, preserve the cranberry bogs and the wide expanse of sand and tide and sky.

The lighthouse, built of red brick, is not open to visitors. It flashes its four lights, three white and one red: a welcome and a warning.

THE FERRY PULLED OUT OF THE SLIP and she was on it. Mary watched Woods Hole disappear behind her. The Steamship Authority and the large grey buildings of the Marine Institute grew smaller and then were altogether gone. The ferry swung out into open water, carrying its cargo of cars and people, trucks, and mailbags. Mary bought a cup of coffee at the concession stand in the creaky lounge area, which smelled of lead paint, hot dogs, and the possibility of being seasick. As always, she was amused by the instructions to the crew of the vessel in case of atomic attack. It amazed her even now that people really believed they could survive, or that measures like "hose the radioactive material off the deck" were considered more than joke.

She made her way up on deck and selected two deck chairs, one as a seat and one for her feet, and stowed her luggage on the rack. She had only a small suitcase and a backpack full of books, for she'd acquired little, wintering in Boston. Sea gulls followed in the ferry wake, and a few children hung over the rail, eagerly holding potato chips or bits of bread aloft, hoping to entice a gull into feeding from their hands, and hoping the birds could distinguish between the snack and their fingers. Mary smelled the sea, saw the white sails dotting the water, heard the buoy clang. Her jaw relaxed and the small muscles in her neck loosened.

After a while, she went back down into the hold again to find the women's bathroom. Here everything again was creaky metal. All that was left of her graffiti lipstick was the small stub; she would have to get another. Still, she wrote on the wall in a bold hand, quoting Patti Smith from memory: I DON'T FUCK MUCH WITH THE PAST BUT I FUCK PLENTY WITH THE FUTURE. She threw out the stub of lipstick and went back up on deck.

Sunlight dazzled the water, ions tickled her nose, and when the ferry whistled she almost jumped out of her skin. They glided into the dock of the Harbor. She was home. Once actually at home, she was confronted with the shack, which was a mess. The paint was peeling and the ground was strewn with branches and debris that had come down in unusually high winter storms. Mary fished her key out of the anachronistic milk box, let herself in, and began an unpremeditated frenzy of housecleaning on the chaotic interior. The shack had many idiosyncrasies, simultaneously irritating and charming. It was one large room — crowded for two messy people, but fine for one neat one. It had a sleeping loft reached by a small ladder, a yellow kitchen table with four mismatched chairs, a rocker, a wood-burning stove that dominated one corner, a sink with a drain but no running water, counters and shelves used as a pantry, a miniscule refrigerator under the sink, and a hip bath. Although the cabin was wired for electricity and had a toaster and hot plate, it was cluttered with hurricane lamps and candles. The power was erratic; the only source of water was a cold outdoor tap. The only luxury was a toilet, which actually worked most of the time, but this was located in a detached closet that sat off the porch, and it was freezing in winter. Mary hauled her water in two dented tin buckets, but preparing a full bath was a chore, and she often visited her mother for a hot shower.

She took up the rag rugs and beat them violently until their pale colors reappeared. Then she swept and mopped the floor, scrubbed the sink and surfaces, and threw out the trash. She also threw out everything of Joe's that he had left behind — ashtrays, fishing lures, motorcycle magazines, rolling papers, a ratty pair of sneakers, an old work shirt, and a perfectly good tie clip. She wanted the place to be completely her own now, and she aired out the clean sheets with their design of clouds and rainbows. The sleeping loft had luminous stars pasted on the ceiling, the kind from the planetarium that lit up children's bedrooms at night. She and Joe had happily pasted them there, but she allowed them to stay. Once clean, she arranged the shack to her liking, grouped the smooth sea stones and boat-shaped shells on the windowsill, filled a jam

jar with daisies, and put all her books with "Zen" in the title
on a makeshift bookshelf of bricks and boards.
Then she wrote out a list on a big sheet of paper:

THINGS TO DO
bank
library — Marge Piercy, Willa Cather, cookbooks
check for old restaurant job back
do laundry
garden?
    rototiller — borrow
    lime
    manure
    peas
    pole beans
    tomatoes?
    corn?
    zucchini
    basil
    mint
    parsley
    marigolds
    lettuce — get flats
    green onions
bicycle pump
diaphragm cream — hope springs eternal
Vitamin C
oatmeal soap
sun tan lotion
call June
call Sarah
post office — start delivery
food shop
toilet paper
paper towels
call Alta
garden gloves — Matty
call Therese
newspaper
facial mask
get car out of Sal's garage

Mary's shack had no phone, but here again she could use the one at Matty's. No sooner did she return to the Island than she remembered that she had friends there, friends she had ignored all winter but who would still greet her with love. There was June, her oldest friend from junior high school, who was now married with two babies, who was straight and boring but sweet and familiar, and in some basic way indispensable. Then there was Alta, so tall, thin, and exotic, with three earrings in each ear, a black woman usually dressed in bright flowing ensembles, wildly layered, a skirt over pants or a shawl over scarves, a yoga teacher who worked in a boutique and whom Mary had met when she was moonlighting as a waitress. And Sarah, the earth mama who was actually from New York City, Jewish, a summer person who had simply not left one summer, who raised fancy poultry and worked as a Town Hall clerk, whose long brown hair and militant non-monogamy and avowed bisexuality kept her permanently in romantic hot water.

Each friend had her particular uses. June was good for calming conversations about where to put in the strawberry plants, for July 4th picnics, for going bra shopping, for Island gossip. Alta was perfect for trading a back rub, for walking on the beach at night, for astrological updates, for herbal tea and cosmic gossip. Each had drawbacks, though. Mary couldn't tell June the truth all the time, or rely on Alta, who sometimes retreated into a private, exclusive mood. Sarah was good for almost everything, except that she gave terrible advice on affairs of the heart. It was her belief that one should add rather than subtract, a view not always shared by all her lovers. Still, Sarah had a warm heart and a willing ear, and she always had tickets for some bizarre dance performance on the beach, a shellfish license and a clambake, an invitation to a party, and a few cute ex-friends she could fix you up with.

However, before Mary called her friends, she ran into Joe at the supermarket.

"Hi," she said, and smiled stupidly.

"Hi," he said. They embraced awkwardly. "So how ya doin'?"

"Okay, okay. I was in Boston for the winter and now I'm back. How are you?"

"Yeah, I heard you were in Beantown. Celtics lost again, those bastards. I'm okay."

Mary felt embarrassed by this moronic conversation. Had they always been this stiff? Obviously not, but she couldn't remember. Then he asked if he could take her to dinner, and her hunger got the better of her.

"Let's just stop by my place first, I have to shower and stuff," said Joe.

His apartment was in an ugly new garden complex, in the small area of town zoned for multiple dwellings. It had four rooms with wall-to-wall green carpeting and almost no furniture.

"You must be doing pretty well to have a place like this."

"Naw, this is just a winter rental, dirt cheap. In fact, I'm out on my ass again in two weeks. Tell me if you hear about any place that's open."

Was he trying to move back in with her? It would be just like him. "Are you still seeing Molly?" she asked.

"Molly? Yeah. She's an okay lady. Right now she's visiting her folks on the mainland."

So that was why he'd been so quick to invite her over. And he didn't ask if she was seeing anybody. Did she look that lonely?

Joe came out of the shower, nothing but a towel wrapped around his waist. She examined him critically. He was a handsome man, dark, broad, almost black hair and eyes inherited from his Portuguese grandmother. He had a heart pierced with swords tattooed on his right arm.

"Want some coke?" he asked.

"Sure." Why not? He took out a tin foil packet of what looked to be about half an ounce and started messing around with the mirror and razor blade.

"Pretty pure stuff," he said. So he was dealing again; that was the only way he could possibly afford it. Well, it wasn't her problem anymore. He cut the cocaine in fat lines on the mirror, rolled up a dollar bill and passed it to her. She snorted a line in each nostril and then got a glass of water and sniffed some of that too. Silently, they passed the mirror back and forth. She did another two lines. She was getting buzzed, very buzzed. Her body felt heavy and then light. She felt wrapped in warmth, but her head was completely clear.

"We could stay here," said Joe. "I mean, I've got some steaks and potatoes, even wine." They reached for each other. She grabbed his chest and they kissed and fell on the floor. She was on top of him, kissing his cocaine-metallic mouth and he was holding her breasts and gently pulling the nipples, the way she'd taught him. They'd been doing this to each other for almost fifteen years; they'd been married and she knew how to make love to him and he to her. It was comforting, exciting, and yet when they were done she couldn't imagine why she had begun. He felt like a stranger, a familiar stranger. She didn't wait for him to cook the steaks. She went home, still stoned, driving her old blue VW, the one without registration or tail lights, abstractedly, and parked it in its accustomed place outside the shack. She would be glad when she could shower, take out her diaphragm, which she had taken to carrying around in her pack; she would be glad when it was morning. She curled up in the sleeping loft and watched the luminous paper stars flicker until she slept.

The weekend of Elizabeth's wedding the weather was perfect, clear and bright, with a cool breeze off the sea. Matty had the house cleaned, called the caterers one last time, had the nursery send up more pots of flowers. It was to be a smallish garden party wedding, with the ceremony under the trees and the reception on the deck and in the garden, but the last-minute acceptances had put the guest list at over seventy-five people, and Matty was frantically overseeing the details. Jed was in charge of the band, Jed's father the liquor, Therese would make the signs to the house and direct the parking, Cathy had promised to chat up all the old ladies present, and Mary was to run up- and down-island on last-minute errands. The minister was non-denominational but presumably legitimate, hailing from Harvard Divinity School. The guests were predominantly old Island friends, customers, neighbors, along with the young graduate school crowd of Jed and Elizabeth's, plus a handful of Jed's relatives, and Elizabeth's cousins from Portland.

The night before the wedding, all of Matty's four daughters slept together under her roof. Cathy and John, as befitting a properly married couple, had the official guest room with bath. The moon was full and it turned the night, the woods, the world, a startling white-blue. John pulled Cathy to him and whispered in her ear: "It's a full moon. Let's do what the rabbits and skunks and shellfish are doing!" And so they did. Hours past midnight the moonlight seemed to grow even brighter, and the round white face of the moon came even closer to the house, as if it might look through one of the picture windows at all the sleepers in their various beds. Cathy woke suddenly. She couldn't sleep, and put on her white cotton robe and crept outside barefoot. There, on a deck chair, looking at the moon, was her mother Matty. They smiled at each other and Cathy sat down companionably at her feet. The low branches of the scrub, pine, and oak were lit up in the moonlight so they could see each individual twig and leaf. The folding chairs were arranged on the lawn for the next day's ceremony.

And then they saw them, the two figures that came hesitantly out of the woods. Almost solid, they were a man and a woman, two early wedding guests, not trespassers. Cathy and Matty could recognize the figures in the clear moonlight. The man was Al, neatly dressed in his light summer suit and carrying a straw panama hat. With him was Muriel, Jed's mother. Matty was relieved to see that she wasn't wearing her bathing suit this time, but was properly dressed in a nice blue cocktail dress, although she was still carrying her sandals in her hand. Slowly the ghosts looked around, and then gently, as if carried by the waft of a breeze, settled down expectantly in two of the front row chairs.

"They came!" breathed Cathy.

"For the wedding," said Matty softly and she stroked her youngest daughter's hair.

Toward morning, the birds — jays, robins, chickadees, warblers — burst into their mid-summer cacophony and daylight paled the windows of the house. Therese woke from a dream and turned to look at Lu's sleeping face. Then she began to wake her by nibbling on her neck and giving her butterfly kisses with her eyelashes. Sleepily, Lu turned to her, and easily they made love: fingers, tongues, juice.

"You think this is a dream, you're still asleep, you won't even remember who I am in the morning," whispered Therese, to tease her.

But Lu just mumbled "Uh" and pulled the covers back up over her head. It wasn't even six A.M. yet, and Therese went back to sleep.

In some strange leap of acceptance Matty had put Therese and Lu up together in the double bed of the attic spare room. She had even laid out fresh towels for them and a bar of sweet smelling soap.

"I told you she knows about us," said Lu triumphantly. "She knows and she doesn't mind."

Therese was not so sure. "You think she knows consciously? I mean, it isn't just because we're roommates?"

"Therese! She saw us kissing on the deck yesterday afternoon when we didn't think anybody was home. She saw us kissing and then she gave us a room with a double bed. And besides, she knows you're coming to San Francisco with me."

"Maybe."

"Maybe what? Maybe your mother knows we are lovers or maybe you're coming with me this fall?"

"I'm coming with you," said Therese.

Mary and Elizabeth were sleeping together on the convertible couch in the living room. Jed was sleeping at his father's summer house; some last-minute sense of decorum or superstition had led him and Elizabeth to sleep apart the night before the wedding. All night long Mary and Elizabeth had tossed and turned in unison, bumping into each other, fighting over the covers. But the way Elizabeth smelled in sleep was very comforting to Mary. It reminded her of when Elizabeth was born.

The bride's and bridesmaids' dresses hung in the closet, neatly pressed and ready to wear. Elizabeth had chosen a cream-colored dress trimmed in lilac. It had a rather Edwardian feel, with a dropped waist and a lacy bodice. She was also going to wear a large straw hat with a veil. The whole ensemble made her feel delightful, literary. Matty, who had remained neutral throughout most of the wedding plans, saying it was Elizabeth's day, had suddenly become crazy and insisted that Elizabeth have her hair done and had also ordered a bridal bouquet of violets and mimosa. She felt a rush of warmth toward Elizabeth that was difficult to express or understand, for Elizabeth was her least favorite daughter.

And yet here she was, the third daughter to marry and yet Matty's first, and probably last, bride.

Elizabeth had simply told her sisters to buy lilac for their bridesmaid dresses. She hoped this was a way for them to avoid the cost of buying some flimsy nothing they would only wear once. Cathy had obligingly bought a bridesmaidy Laura Ashley dress. It almost matched her favorite sheets and was in a predominantly lilac floral. She thought she was getting too old to wear this kind of thing, but she enjoyed it anyway. In contrast, Mary had bumbled around Cambridge's cheaper boutiques until she found a flowing ethnic dress that was at least light purple if not lilac. It was sheer enough to need a slip, which she had to borrow from Matty at the last moment. When Therese had heard that she needed a dress she had thrown a small fit, cursing at her reflection in the bathroom mirror and throwing a bar of soap at the two offended cats who were watching her. Then, she had briskly taken herself off to Jordan Marsh and spent several hundred dollars on the first dress she tried on: a two-piece lavender silk, cut in a sort of Grecian tunic style. In it, Therese looked like some Amazon goddess; everyone was forced to agree she looked quite simply gorgeous.

When Mary woke up next to Elizabeth she was grateful that she had a bedmate, and she was acutely aware that she would be the only one of the sisters to attend the wedding dateless, mateless. It had been a long time since she had told anyone that she loved them. She decided to try, and settled upon Therese, who was naked and brushing her teeth at the kitchen sink.

"I love you, Therese," said Mary, coming up behind her and embracing her fervently.

"Blub," said Therese, splitting out toothpaste and rinsing her mouth.

"I love you, and I think you look gorgeous in your new dress," said Mary.

"I love you too," said Therese, and her kiss smelled of mouthwash.

A few hours before the wedding Elizabeth lost all pretense to calm, and began running around, tidying things at random and staring cross-eyed at herself in every mirror.

"Plates! We need more cake plates. And forks! Oh my God, I'm never going to make it. I need valium. Nobody has any Valium?"

No one did; Cathy suggested a hot bath and Mary, glad to escape, offered to run the car into town and pick up an excess of plates.

Coming back up the Island, her errand accomplished, Mary passed her favorite cemetery and stopped the car on the dirt shoulder of the road. She got out and entered the cemetery formally through a green wicket gate. Then she lay down in the long grass, with one of the old slate graves as a headstone, and idly picked a dandelion apart. She lay in the grass and looked up at the sky. The burying ground was in a field of sunflowers, those awkwardly large, graceful turners after the sun. The field was in the center of the Island; the Island was in the center of the ocean, in the middle of a blue sea full of sharks and whales, treasure and shipwreck, drowned sailors and microscopic protozoa. She lay in the center of everything and felt the field turn toward the sun, the globe spin, the long arm of the universe swing out into space, and beyond that the void was turning, too.

There was no death. Then she got up, brushed the grass off her pants, and went back up-island to the wedding.

About The Author

Miriam Sagan was born in New York City, educated at Harvard and Boston University, and lived on the coastal extremes of San Francisco and Martha's Vineyard. She currently lives in Santa Fe, New Mexico with her husband and daughter.

She is the author of a dozen books, chapbooks, and cassettes including *Aegean Doorway* (Zephyr, 1984), *Spilling Marmalade* (Pectin Audio, 1987) and *True Body* (Parallax, 1991).